PENGUIN CLASSICS ⟨🐧⟩ DELUXE EDITION

THE BOOK OF IMAGINARY BEINGS

One of the greatest writers of the twentieth century, JORGE LUIS BORGES (1899–1986) published numerous collections of poems, essays, and fiction. Director of the National Library of Buenos Aires from 1955 to 1973, Borges was awarded the degree of Doctor of Letters, honoris causa, from both Columbia and Oxford universities. He received various literary awards over the course of his career, including the International Publishers' Prize (which he shared with Samuel Beckett in 1961), the Jerusalem Prize, and the Alfonso Reyes Prize.

ANDREW HURLEY has translated the *Collected Fictions* of Borges as well as works by Reinaldo Arenas and Arturo Pérez-Reverte, among others.

PETER SÍS has received five *New York Times Book Review* Best Illustrated Book of the Year Awards, a Society of Illustrators Gold Medal, and a Caldecott Honor. He was named a MacArthur Fellow in 2003.

JORGE LUIS BORGES

The Book of Imaginary Beings

with Margarita Guerrero

Translated by ANDREW HURLEY
Illustrated by PETER SÍS

PENGUIN BOOKS

PENGUIN BOOKS

Published by the Penguin Group

Penguin Group (USA) Inc., 375 Hudson Street, New York, New York 10014, U.S.A. • Penguin Group (Canada), 90 Eglinton Avenue East, Suite 700, Toronto, Ontario, Canada M4P 2Y3 (a division of Pearson Penguin Canada Inc.) • Penguin Books Ltd, 80 Strand, London WC2R 0RL, England • Penguin Ireland, 25 St Stephen's Green, Dublin 2, Ireland (a division of Penguin Books Ltd) • Penguin Group (Australia), 250 Camberwell Road, Camberwell, Victoria 3124, Australia (a division of Pearson Australia Group Pty Ltd) • Penguin Books India Pvt Ltd, 11 Community Centre, Panchsheel Park, New Delhi – 110 017, India • Penguin Group (NZ), 67 Apollo Drive, Rosedale, Auckland 0632, New Zealand (a division of Pearson New Zealand Ltd) • Penguin Books (South Africa) (Pty) Ltd, 24 Sturdee Avenue, Rosebank, Johannesburg 2196, South Africa

Penguin Books Ltd, Registered Offices: 80 Strand, London WC2R 0RL, England

This edition first published in the United States of America by Viking Penguin, a member of Penguin Group (USA) Inc. 2005
Published in Penguin Books 2006

25th Printing

THE LIBRARY OF CONGRESS HAS CATALOGED THE HARDCOVER EDITION AS FOLLOWS:
Borges, Jorge Luis.
[Libro de los seres imaginarios. English]
The Book of Imaginary Beings / Jorge Luis Borges, with Margarita Guerrero; translated by Andrew Hurley; illustrated by Peter Sís.
p.   cm.
ISBN 0-670-89180-0 (hc.)
ISBN 978-0-14-303993-8 (pbk.)
1. Animals, Mythical.   I. Guerrero, Margarita.   II. Hurley, Andrew.   III. Title.
GR825.B613 2005
398'.469—dc22   2005042250

Printed in the United States of America
Set in Aldus
Designed by Francesca Belanger

Contents

Foreword to the First Edition:
An Anthology of Fantastic Zoology

A child is taken for the first time to the zoo. That child may grow up to be you or me, or, conversely, we may once have been that child but have forgotten. At the zoo, that terrible "zoological garden," the child sees living animals he has never seen before—jaguars, vultures, buffalo, and, strangest of all, giraffes. He sees for the first time the confused variety of the animal kingdom, and the spectacle, far from alarming or frightening him, delights him. It delights him so much, in fact, that a trip to the zoo becomes part of the "fun" of childhood, or what passes for fun. How is one to explain this common and yet mysterious occurrence?

We can, of course, deny it. We can tell ourselves that children brusquely led into that garden become, twenty years down the line, neurotic, and the truth is, there's not a child who has not discovered the zoo and not an adult who is not, when carefully examined, discovered to be neurotic. Or we may assert that the child is, by definition, a discoverer, and that discovering the camel is no more remarkable than discovering mirrors, or water, or stairs. We may assert that the child trusts his parents, those who take him into that place filled with animals. Besides, the stuffed tiger on his bed and the tiger in the encyclopedia have prepared him to look without fear upon the tiger of flesh and blood. Plato (should he join in this discussion) would tell us that the child has already seen the tiger, in the world of archetypes, and that now, seeing it, he but *recognizes* it. Schopenhauer (still more startlingly) would say that the child looks without fear on tigers because he knows that he is the tigers and the tigers are he, or, more precisely, that tigers and he are of one essence—Will.

Let us move now from the zoo of reality to the zoo of mythology, that zoological garden whose fauna is comprised not of lions but of sphinxes and gryphons and centaurs. The population of this second zoo should by all rights exceed that of the first, since a monster is nothing but a combination of elements taken from real creatures, and the combinatory possibilities border on the infinite. In the centaur, horse and man are mingled; in the Minotaur, bull and man (Dante imagined it with the face of a human and the body of a bull). Following this lead, it seems to us, any number of monsters, combinations of fish, bird, and reptile, might be produced—the only limit being our own ennui or revulsion. That, however, never happens; the monsters that we make would be stillborn, thank God. In the last pages of *The Temptation of St. Anthony*, Flaubert brought together all sorts of medieval and classical monsters, and even (his commentators tell us) attempted to invent some of his own; the total is not great, and those creatures that exert power over mankind's imagination are really very few. Readers browsing through our own anthology will see that the zoology attributable to dreams is in fact considerably more modest than that attributable to God.

We do not know what the dragon *means*, just as we do not know the meaning of the universe, but there is something in the image of the dragon that is congenial to man's imagination, and thus the dragon arises in many latitudes and ages. It is, one might say, a *necessary* monster, not some ephemeral and casual creature like the chimæra or the catoblepas.

We would add that we have no illusions that this book, perhaps the first of its kind, contains within its covers every fantastic animal. We have pored through the classics and through Oriental literature, but we are perfectly aware that the subject we have undertaken is infinite.

We have deliberately excluded from this anthology legends concerning human transformations—the werewolf and the like.

We wish to express our gratitude for the kind help of Leonor Guerrero de Coppola, Alberto D'Aversa, and Rafael López Pellegri.

—J.L.B.–M.G.

Martínez, January 29, 1954

Foreword to the 1967 Edition

The title of this book would justify the inclusion of Prince Hamlet, the point, the line, the plane, the hypercube, all generic nouns, and, perhaps, each one of us and the divinity as well. In sum, virtually the entire universe. We have, however, abided by that which is immediately suggested by the phrase "imaginary beings," and have compiled a volume of the strange creatures that man's fantasy has engendered throughout time and space.

We do not know what the dragon *means,* just as we do not know the meaning of the universe, but there is something in the image of the dragon that is congenial to man's imagination, and thus the dragon arises in many latitudes and ages.

A book of this nature is necessarily incomplete; each new edition is the core of future editions, which may be multiplied to infinity. We invite its eventual readers in Colombia or Paraguay to send us the names, reliable descriptions, and most conspicuous habits of their own local monsters.

Like all miscellanies, like those inexhaustible volumes by Robert Burton, Fraser, or Pliny, *The Book of Imaginary Beings* has not been written for consecutive reading. Our wish would be that the curious dip into it from time to time in much the way one visits the changing forms revealed by a kaleidoscope.

The sources of this "anthology" are many; we have indicated them for each article. We regret any inadvertent omission.

—J.L.B.–M.G.
Martínez, September 1967

The Book of Imaginary Beings

The A Bao A Qu

If one wishes to gaze upon the most marvelous landscape in the world, one must go to the topmost story of the Tower of Victory in Chitor. There, one will find a circular terrace from which one commands a view clear to the horizon, all around. A spiral staircase leads up to this terrace, and yet the only persons who dare venture up the stairs are those who do not believe in the fable, which goes like this:

On the staircase of the Tower of Victory, there has lived from the beginning of time the A Bao A Qu, which is sensitive to the virtues possessed by human souls. It lives upon the first step in a state of lethargy, and comes to conscious life only when someone climbs the stairs. The vibration of the person as he approaches infuses the creature with life, and an inward light begins to glow within it. At the same time, its body and its virtually translucent skin begin to ripple and stir. When a person climbs the stairs, the A Bao A Qu follows almost on the person's heels, climbing up after him, clinging to the edge of the curved treads worn down by the feet of generations of pilgrims. On each step, the creature's color grows more intense, its form becomes more perfect, and the light that emanates from it shines ever brighter. Proof of the creature's sensitivity is the fact that it achieves its perfect form only when it reaches the topmost step, when the person who has climbed the stairs has become a fully evolved and realized spirit. In all other cases, the A Bao A Qu remains as though paralyzed, midway up the staircase, its body incomplete, its color still undefined, its light unsteady. When it cannot achieve its perfect form, the A Bao A Qu suffers great pain, and its moaning is a barely

perceptible murmur similar to the whisper of silk. But when the man or woman that revives the creature is filled with purity, the A Bao A Qu is able to reach the topmost step, completely formed and radiating a clear blue light. Its return to life is brief, however, for when the pilgrim descends the stairs again, the A Bao A Qu rolls down to the first step once more, where, now muted and resembling some faded picture with vague outlines, it awaits the next visitor to the Tower. The creature becomes fully visible only when it reaches the midpoint of the staircase, where the extensions of its body (which, like little arms, help it to climb the stairs) take on clear definition. There are those who say that it can see with its entire body, and that its skin feels like that of a peach. Down through all the centuries, the A Bao A Qu has reached perfection only once.

Captain Richard Francis Burton records the legend of the A Bao A Qu in one of the notes to his version of *The Thousand and One Nights.*

Abtu and Anet

According to Egyptian mythology, Abtu and Anet are two identical sacred fish that swim along before the ship carrying the sun god Ra, in order to warn him against danger. During the day, the ship travels through the sky, from east to west; at night, it sails below the earth, in the opposite direction.

The Monster Acheron

Only one man ever saw the monster Acheron, and that, but a single time. The event took place in the twelfth century in the city of Cork; the original text of the story, written in the old Irish language, has been lost, but a Benedictine monk in Regensburg translated it into Latin, and from that translation the story passed into many languages—among others, Swedish and Spanish. Fifty-odd manuscripts still exist of the Latin text, all agreeing on the essential points of the story; *Visio Tundali* ("The Vision of Tundale") is its title, and it is considered a source for Dante.

Let us begin with the word "Acheron." In the tenth book of *The Odyssey,* Acheron is a river that flows from Hades; it runs through the western borders of the habitable earth. Its name reechoes in *The Æneid,* in Lucan's *Pharsalia,* and in Ovid's *Metamorphoses.* Dante records it in one line as: "*Su la trista riviera d'Acheronte.*"

One legend makes Acheron a castigated Titan; another later tradition locates it not far from the South Pole, under the constellations of the antipodes. The Etruscans possessed "Domesday books" that taught divination and "Acherontic books" that taught the paths of the soul after the body's death. In time, "Acheron" came to mean "the underworld."

Tundale was a young Irish nobleman, well brought up and brave, but of certain dubious habits. He fell ill in the house of a lady friend, and for three days and three nights was thought to be dead, except that some warmth was still detectable nearabouts his heart. When he regained consciousness, he said that his guardian angel had shown him the regions of the netherworld. Of the many marvels he saw there, the one that interests us here is the monster Acheron.

Acheron was larger than a mountain. Its eyes shot forth flames and its mouth was so enormous that nine thousand men would fit inside. Two of the condemned, like pillars or caryatids, held the monster's jaws open; one was upright, the other upside-down. The beast had three gullets; all vomited forth inextinguishable fire. From the beast's belly there issued the constant lamentations of the numberless condemned who had been devoured. The devils told Tundale that the monster's name was Acheron. The guardian angel disappeared and Tundale was dragged down with all the others. Inside the monster he found tears, fog and mist, the cracking and crushing sound of teeth, fire, an unbearable burning sensation, a glacial cold, dogs, bears, lions, and snakes. In this legend, Hell is an animal with other animals inside it.

In 1758, Emanuel Swedenborg wrote: "I have not been allowed to see the general shape of Hell, but they tell me that just as Heaven has human form, so Hell has the form of a demon."

The Amphisbæna

T he *Pharsalia* enumerates the real or imaginary serpents that Cato's soldiers confronted in the deserts of Africa; there they found the Parias, which "walks upright like a walking-stick," the Jaculus, or "flying javelin-snake," and "the dangerous two-headed Amphisbæna." Pliny describes the Amphisbæna in virtually the same words, save that regarding the creature's two heads he adds: "as though one mouth were too little for the discharge of all its venom." Brunetto Latini's *Thesaurus*—that encyclopedia which Latini, in the seventh circle of the Inferno, recommended to his former student—is less sententious and more straightforward: "The Amphisbæna is a serpent with two heads, one in its meet place and the other in the creature's tail; and with both can it bite, and it runs most lightly, and its eyes gleam like live coals." In the seventeenth century, Sir Thomas Browne observed that there is no animal without the "six positions of body" ("*infra, supra, ante, retro, dextrorsum, sinistrorsum*") and he denied that the Amphisbæna could actually exist, for "there is no inferiour or former part in this animall, for the senses being placed at both extreames, doe make both ends anteriour." In Greek, "Amphisbæna" means "that which goes in two directions." In the Antilles and in certain parts of the New World, the name is applied to a reptile commonly known as the "double walker," the "two-headed serpent," or the "mother of ants." It is claimed that ants serve and nourish it, and also that if it is cut into two pieces, the pieces will join together again.

Pliny praised the medicinal virtues of the Amphisbæna.

Swedenborg's Angels

During the last twenty-five years of his scholarly life, the eminent philosopher and man of science Emanuel Swedenborg (1688–1772) made his home in London. As the English are a taciturn people, Swedenborg fell into the habit of conversing with demons and angels. He was even allowed by God to visit the underworld and chat with its inhabitants. Christ had said that if a soul were to enter into Heaven, it must be just; Swedenborg added that it must be intelligent; Blake was to stipulate some time later that it must be artistic. Swedenborg's Angels are the souls that have chosen Heaven. They have no need of words; all one Angel has to do is think of another, and that other Angel will appear beside him. Two people who have loved one another on earth make a single Angel. Their world is ruled by love; each Angel is a Heaven. Their form is that of a perfect human; so is the form of Heaven. Wherever Angels look—north, south, east, or west—they always see God before them. They are first and foremost theologians; their greatest pleasure lies in prayer and the discussion of spiritual problems. The things of earth are symbols of the things of Heaven: the sun corresponds to the deity. There is no time in Heaven. Things' appearances change to correspond to states of emotion; each Angel's clothing shines in proportion to its intelligence. In Heaven, the rich continue to be richer than the poor, since they are accustomed to wealth. In Heaven, objects, furniture, and cities are more concrete and complex than they are on our earth; colors are more varied and more vivid. Angels of English descent are drawn toward politics; Jews, to the jewel trade; Germans carry books about with them that they consult before answering a question. Since Muslims are in the habit of worshipping Mohammed, God has provided them with an Angel who pretends to be the Prophet. The pleasures of Paradise are withheld from the poor in spirit and all ascetics, because they would not understand them.

An Animal Dreamed by Kafka

It is the animal with the big tail, a tail many yards long and like a fox's brush. How I should like to get my hand on this tail some time, but it is impossible, the animal is constantly moving about, the tail is constantly being flung this way and that. The animal resembles a kangaroo, but not as to the face, which is flat almost like a human face, and small and oval; only its teeth have any power of expression, whether they are concealed or bared. Sometimes I have the feeling that the animal is trying to tame me. What other purpose could it have in withdrawing its tail when I snatch at it, and then again, waiting calmly until I am tempted again, and then leaping away once more?

—Franz Kafka, *Hochzeitsvorbereitungen auf dem Lande,* 1953.

An Animal Dreamed by C. S. Lewis

The noise was very loud now and the thicket very dense so that he could not see a yard ahead, when the music stopped suddenly. There was a sound of rustling and broken twigs and he made hastily in that direction, but found nothing. He had almost decided to give up the search when the song began again a little farther away. Once more he made after it; once more the creature stopped singing and evaded him. He must have played thus at hide-and-seek with it for the best part of an hour before his search was rewarded.

Treading delicately during one of the loudest bursts of music he at last saw through the flowery branches a black something. Standing still whenever it stopped singing, and advancing with great caution whenever it began again, he stalked it for ten minutes. At last it was in full view, and singing, and ignorant that it was watched. It sat upright like a dog, black and sleek and shiny, but its shoulders were high above Ransom's head, and the forelegs on which they were pillared were like young trees and the wide soft pads on which they rested were large as those of a camel. The enormous rounded belly was white, and far up above the shoulders the neck rose like that of a horse. The head was in profile from where Ransom stood—the mouth wide open as it sang of joy in thick-coming trills, and the music almost visibly rippled in its glossy throat. He stared in wonder at the wide liquid eyes and the quivering, sensitive nostrils. Then the creature stopped, saw him, and darted away, and stood, now a few paces distant, on all four legs, not much smaller than a young elephant, swaying a long bushy tail. It was the first thing in Perelandra which seemed to show any fear of man. Yet it was not fear. When he called to it it came nearer. It put its velvet nose into his hand and endured his touch; but almost at once it darted back and, bending its long neck, buried its head in its paws. He could make no headway with it, and when at length it retreated out of sight he did not follow it. To do so would have seemed an injury to its fawn-like shyness, to the yielding softness of its expression, its evident wish to be for ever a sound and only a sound in the thickest centre of untravelled woods. He resumed his journey: a few seconds later the song broke out behind him, louder and lovelier than before, as if in a paean of rejoicing at its recovered privacy.

The beasts of that kind have no milk and always what they bring forth is suckled by the she-beast of another kind. She is great and beautiful and dumb, and till the young singing beast is weaned it is among her whelps and is subject to her. But when it is grown it becomes the most delicate and glorious of all beasts and goes from her. And she wonders at its song.

—C. S. Lewis, *Perelandra.*

The Animal Dreamed by Poe

In *The Narrative of Arthur Gordon Pym of Nantucket*, published in 1838, Edgar Allan Poe peopled the islands of Antarctica with an astonishing, albeit believable, fauna. In Chapter 18, we read:

> We also picked up a bush, full of red berries, like those of the hawthorn, and the carcass of a singular-looking land animal. It was three feet in length, and but six inches in height, with four very short legs, the feet armed with long claws of a brilliant scarlet, and resembling coral in substance. The body was covered with a straight silky hair, perfectly white. The tail was peaked like that of a rat, and about a foot and a half long. The head resembled a cat's with the exception of the ears—these were flapped like the ears of a dog. The *teeth* were of the same brilliant scarlet as the claws.

No less remarkable was the water of those antipodean lands:

> On account of the singular character of the water, we refused to taste it, supposing it to be polluted. . . . I am at a loss to give a distinct idea of the nature of this liquid, and cannot do so without many words. Although it flowed with rapidity in all declivities where common water would do so, yet never, except when falling in a cascade, had it the customary appearance of *limpidity*. . . . Where little declivity was found, it bore resemblance, as regards consistency, to a thick infusion of gum Arabic in common water.

But this was only the least remarkable of its extraordinary qualities. It was *not* colorless, nor was it of any one uniform color—presenting to the eye, as it flowed, every possible shade of purple, like the hues of a changeable silk. . . . Upon collecting a basinful, and allowing it to settle thoroughly, we perceived that the whole mass of liquid was made up of a number of distinct veins, each of a distinct hue, and that these veins did not commingle. . . . Upon passing the blade of a knife athwart the veins, the water closed over it immediately, as with us, and also, in withdrawing it, all traces of the passage of the knife were instantly obliterated. If, however, the blade was passed down accurately between the two veins, a perfect separation was effected, which the power of cohesion did not immediately rectify.

—Edgar Allan Poe, *The Narrative of Arthur Gordon Pym.*

Two Metaphysical Animals

The problem of the origin of ideas contributes two curious creatures to the fauna of mankind's imagination. One was invented sometime in the mid–eighteenth century; the other, a hundred years later.

The first creature is Condillac's "sentient statue." Descartes professed the doctrine of innate ideas; in order to refute him, Étienne Bonnot de Condillac imagined a marble statue shaped like a man's body and animated by a soul that has never perceived, never thought. Condillac begins by endowing the statue with a single sense—smell, perhaps the least complex of the five senses. The fragrance of jasmine is the beginning of the statue's biography; for one instant, there shall be nothing in all the universe but that odor. More precisely, that odor shall *be* the universe, which a second later will be the fragrance of a rose, and then a carnation. Let there be a single odor in the consciousness of the statue, and we have attention; let a fragrance last beyond the moment when the stimulus has passed, and we have memory; let one impression in the present and one from the past occupy the statue's attention, and we have comparison; let the statue perceive analogies and differences, and we have judgment; let comparison and judgment occur again, and we have reflection; let a pleasant memory be more vivid than an unpleasant one, and we have imagination. When the faculties of the Understanding have been engendered, the faculties of the Will must follow—love and hate (attraction and aversion), hope and fear. The awareness of having passed through many states will give the statue an abstract notion of number; the awareness of *being* the odor of carnation yet of *having been* the odor of jasmine will endow it with the idea of Self.

Condillac would then grant his hypothetical man hearing, taste, sight, and, lastly, touch. This last sense reveals to the creature the fact that space exists and that within space, he himself is within a body; sounds, fragrances, and colors will have seemed to him, before that moment, simple variations or modifications of his consciousness.

The allegory we have just retold is titled *Traité des sensations*, and it was published in 1754; for this account of it, we have used the second volume of Bréhier's *Histoire de la philosophie*.

The other creature engendered by the problem of knowledge is Lotze's "hypothetical animal." More solitary than the statue that smells roses and at last becomes a man, this animal has but one sensitive spot on its skin, on the end of an antenna and therefore movable. The structure of this animal prevents it, as one can see, from receiving simultaneous perceptions, but Lotze believed that the ability to retract or project its sensitive antenna was enough to allow the all-but-isolated animal to discover the outside world (without the aid of Kantian categories) and to perceive the difference between a stationary object and a mobile one. Vaihinger admired this fiction; it is contained in the work titled *Medizinische Psychologie*, published in 1852.

Animals That Live in the Mirror

In one of the volumes of the *Lettres edifiantes et curieuses* that appeared in Paris sometime during the first half of the eighteenth century, Father Zallinger, of the Company of Jesus, mentioned the possibility of compiling a catalog of the illusions and errors of the common folk of Canton province. In a preliminary listing, he noted that the Fish was an elusive, gleaming creature that no one had ever touched but that many people believed they had seen in the depths of mirrors. Father Zallinger died in 1736, and the work begun by his pen remained unfinished; one hundred fifty years later, Herbert Allen Giles took up the interrupted labor. According to Giles, belief in the Fish is part of a broader myth, which goes back to the legendary age of the Yellow Emperor.

In those days, the world of mirrors and the world of men were not, as they are now, separate and unconnected. They were, moreover, quite different from one another; neither the creatures nor the colors nor the shapes of the two worlds were the same. The two kingdoms—the specular and the human—lived in peace, and one could pass back and forth through mirrors. One night, however, the people of the mirror invaded this world. Their strength was great, but after many bloody battles, the magic of the Yellow Emperor prevailed. The Emperor pushed back the invaders, imprisoned them within the mirrors, and punished them by making them repeat, as though in a kind of dream, all the actions of their human victors. He stripped them of their strength and their own shape and reduced them to mere servile reflections. One day, however, they will throw off that magical lethargy.

The first to awaken shall be the Fish. In the depths of the mirror, we shall perceive a faint, faint line, and the color of that line will not resemble any other. Then, other forms will begin to awaken. Gradually they will become different from us; gradually they will no longer imitate us; they will break through the barriers of glass or metal, and this time they will not be conquered. Water-creatures will battle alongside mirror-creatures.

In Yunnan province, people speak not of the Fish but rather the Tiger of the Mirror. Others believe that before the invasion, we will hear, from the depths of the mirrors, the sound of arms.

Spherical Animals

The sphere is the most uniform of the solid bodies, inasmuch as every point on its surface is equidistant from its center. For this reason, and because of its "uniform circular motion on the same spot," Plato (*Timæus*, 33) praised the Demiurge's decision to give the world spherical form. The world, in Plato's judgment, was a living being, and in the *Laws* he stated that the planets and stars are living creatures, too, endowed with souls. He gave to our fantastic zoology, then, vast Spherical Animals, and he criticized the slow-witted astronomers who refused to see that the circular movement of celestial bodies was spontaneous and voluntary.

More than five hundred years later, in Alexandria, Origen taught that the blessed were to be reborn in the form of spheres, and that they would roll into eternity.

In the Renaissance, the concept of Heaven as an animal reappeared in Vantini; the Neoplatonist Marsilio Ficino spoke of the hair, teeth, and bones of the earth; and Giordano Bruno felt that the planets were large, peaceable, warm-blooded animals of regular habits, endowed with reason. In the early seventeenth century, Kepler disputed with the English alchemist Robert Fludd over which of the two men had first conceived the notion that the Earth was a living monster, "whose whalelike breathing, corresponding to the states of sleeping and waking, produces the ebb and flow of the sea." The monster's anatomy, its eating habits, its color, its memory, and its imaginative or plastic faculty were studied by Kepler.

In the nineteenth century, the German psychologist Gustav Theodor Fechner (a man praised by William James in *A Pluralis-*

tic Universe) rethought all these ideas, with a kind of naive ingenuity. Those who are able to entertain the notion that the earth, our mother, is an organism—an organism superior to the plant, the animal, and man himself—may examine the devout pages of Fechner's *Zend-Avesta*. There they will read, for example, that the spherical shape of the earth is that of the human eye, which is the most noble part of our body. They will also read that "if the sky is truly the home of angels, then angels must surely be stars, for there are no other inhabitants of the sky."

Six-Legged Antelopes

The Eddas tell us that Odin's gray horse Sleipnir (which travels over land, through the air, and down into the lower world) is endowed with (or encumbered by) eight legs; a Siberian myth attributes six legs to the first Antelopes. With these six legs, the Antelopes were very difficult, even impossible, to overtake; so the divine huntsman Tunk-poj made a pair of special skates from the wood of a sacred tree which creaked incessantly and which had been revealed to him by the barking of a dog. The skates creaked as well, though they traveled with the swiftness of an arrow; to moderate their speed, Tunk-poj fitted them with chocks, which he made with branches from another magical tree. Tunk-poj pursued the Antelope across the entire firmament. Finally, the Antelope, exhausted, fell to the earth and Tunk-poj cut off its two hind legs.

"Men," he said, "are growing smaller and weaker every day. How can they hunt Six-Legged Antelopes if I myself can barely catch them?"

Since that day, Antelopes have had four legs.

The Three-Legged Ass

Pliny reports that Zoroaster, the founder of the religion still professed by the Parsees of Bombay, wrote two million lines of poetry; the Arab historian al-Tabari states that the holy man's complete works, given eternal life by devoted calligraphers, required twelve thousand cowhides. We know that Alexander of Macedonia ordered that the manuscripts in Persepolis be burned, but the fundamental Zoroastrian texts were saved through the remarkable memory of certain priests. Since the ninth century these texts have been complemented by an encyclopedic work called the *Bundahish*, which contains the following passage:

> Regarding the Three-Legged Ass, they say that it stands amid the wide-formed ocean, and that its feet are three, its eyes six, its mouths nine, its ears two, and its horn one; its body is white, its food is spiritual, and it is wholly righteous. And two of its six eyes are in the position of eyes, two on the top of the head, and two in the position of the hump; with the sharpness of those six eyes it overcomes and destroys. Of the nine mouths, three are in the head, three in the hump, and three in the inner part of the flanks; and each mouth is about the size of a cottage. . . . Each one of its three feet, when it is placed on the ground, is as much as a flock of a thousand sheep may lie in when they repose together; and each pastern is so great in its circuit that a thousand men with a thousand horses may pass inside. As for the beast's two ears, it is Mazandaran[*]

*A province of northern Persia.

which they will encompass. Its one horn is like unto gold and hollow, and a thousand branch horns have grown upon it, some befitting a camel, some befitting a horse, some befitting an ox, some befitting an ass, both great and small. With that horn it shall vanquish and it shall put to rout all the vile corruption brought about by the efforts of noxious creatures.

We know that amber is the dung of the Three-Legged Ass. In Mazdeic mythology this beneficent monster is one of the helpers of Ahura Mazda (Ormuzd), the principle of Life, Light, and Truth.

The Bahamut

The fame of the Bahamut reached as far as the deserts of Arabia, where men changed and magnified its image. At first a hippopotamus or an elephant, at last it was transformed into a fish that floats in a bottomless sea; above the fish the men of Arabia pictured a bull, and above the bull a mountain made of ruby, and above the mountain an angel, and above the angel six infernos, and above the infernos the earth, and above the earth seven heavens. Here is the story of this creature, in Lane's translation:

> The earth was, it is said, originally unstable, and therefore God created an angel of immense size and of the utmost strength, and ordered him to go beneath it and place it on his shoulders. . . . But there was no support for his feet: so God created a rock of ruby, . . . and he ordered this rock to stand under the feet of the angel. But there was no support for the rock: wherefore God created a huge bull, with four thousand eyes and the same number of ears, noses, mouths, tongues, and feet; . . . and God, whose name be exalted, ordered this bull to go beneath the rock; and he bore it on his back and his horns. . . . But there was no support for the bull: therefore God, whose name be exalted, created an enormous fish, that no one could look upon on account of its vast size, and the flashing of its eyes, and their greatness; . . . and God, whose name be exalted, commanded the fish to be a support to the feet of the bull. The name of this fish is Bahamoot [Behemoth]. He placed, as its support, water; and under the water,

darkness: and the knowledge of mankind fails as to what is under the darkness.

Another opinion is, that the earth is upon water; the water, upon the rock; the rock, on the back of the bull; the bull, on a bed of sand; the sand, on the fish; the fish, upon a still, suffocating wind; the wind, on a veil of darkness; the darkness, on a mist; and what is beneath the mist is unknown.

So immense and resplendent is the Bahamut that human eyes cannot bear to look upon it. All the seas of the earth, placed in one of the nostrils of its nose, would be no more than a grain of mustard in the midst of the desert. In Night 496 of the Burton's version of the *Thousand and One Nights*, we read that Isa (Jesus) was allowed to see the Bahamut, and when this gift was bestowed upon him he fell down in a swoon, and did not awake from the swoon that had come upon him for three days. Later, we read in addition that beneath the huge fish there is a sea, and beneath the sea, "a vast abyss of air, [and] under the air fire, and under the fire a mighty serpent, by name Falak," in whose mouth lies the Inferno.

The fiction of the rock standing upon the bull, and the bull upon Bahamut, and Bahamut upon something else could well be an illustration of that cosmological proof of the existence of God which argues that every cause requires a prior cause—so that at last, if one is not to go on to infinity, one comes to the necessity of a First Cause.

The Baldanders

The Baldanders (whose name, singular in the German, might be translated "suddenly different" or "suddenly other") was suggested to the Nuremberg shoemaker Hans Sachs by that passage in *The Odyssey* in which Menelaus is attempting to subdue the Egyptian god Proteus, who transforms himself into a lion, a serpent, a panther, an immense wild boar, a tree, and finally, water. Hans Sachs died in 1576; some ninety years later, the Baldanders reappeared in the sixth book of Grimmelshausen's fantasy-picaresque novel *Simplicius Simplicissimus*. In a forest, the hero comes upon a stone statue that he takes for the idol from some old Germanic temple. He touches the statue and the statue tells him that it is Baldanders, and that it can take the shape of a man, an oak tree, a sow, a sausage, a meadow full of clover, dung, a flower, a flowering branch, a mulberry tree, a silk tapestry, and many other things and beings, and then, once more, a man. It attempts to teach Simplicissimus the art "of speaking with things which by their nature are mute, such as chairs and benches, pots and kettles"; it also turns itself into a secretary and writes these words from St. John's Revelations: "I am Alpha and Omega, the beginning and the ending," which are the key to the coded document in which the instructions for that art are written. Baldanders adds that its coat of arms (like the Turk's, though with more justice) is the inconstant moon.

Baldanders is a *successive monster*, a monster in time; the title page of the first edition of Grimmelshausen's novel bears an engraving that portrays a being with the head of a satyr, the torso of a man, the outspread wings of a bird, and the tail of a fish; with one goat's foot and one vulture's claw it stands atop a mound of masks, which might be the individuals of the species. On its belt there hangs a sword; its hands hold an open book, with the figures of a crown, a ship, a chalice, a tower, a baby, a pair of dice, a fool's-cap with bells, and a cannon.

Banshees

No one seems ever to have seen one; they are less a shape than a wailing that lends horror to the nights of Ireland and (according to Sir Walter Scott's *Letters on Demonology and Witchcraft*) the mountain regions of Scotland. Heard outside one's window, they herald the death of some member of the family. It is the peculiar privilege of certain lineages of pure Celtic blood—with no trace of Latin, Saxon, or Norse—to hear them. They are also heard in Wales and Brittany. They belong to the race of elves. Their wailing is known as "keening."

The Basilisk

own through the ages, the Basilisk became more and
more ugly, more and more horrible, but now it is forgotten. Its name means "little king"; Pliny the Elder
(VIII, 33) tells us that the Basilisk was a serpent "with a white
spot on the head, strongly resembling a sort of a diadem." From
the Middle Ages onward, however, it was a crowned, quadrupedal
cock with yellow plumage and great thorny wings; only its tail
was that of a serpent (and it might end in a claw or in another
cock's-head). The change in its image is reflected in a change of
name: by the fourteenth century, Chaucer speaks of the "Basili-
cock." One of the engravings in Aldrovandi's *Natural Historie of
Serpents and Dragons* gives it scales, not feathers, and also portrays it with eight legs.*

What does not change is the fatal virtue of its glance. The
Gorgons' eyes turned all they looked upon to stone; Lucan tells
us that from the blood of one of the Gorgons, the Medusa, all the
serpents of Libya were spawned—the Asp, the Amphisbæna, the
Ammodytes, the Basilisk. The passage may be found in the ninth
book of the *Pharsalia*; here is Robert Graves's translation:

> Medusa is said to have lived in the far west of Africa, at
> the point where the Ocean laps against the hot earth, in a
> wide, untilled, treeless region which she had turned en-
> tirely to stone merely by gazing around her. The story is
> that, when her head was cut off, serpents were bred from

*Like, according to the Younger Edda, the eight legs of Odin's horse Sleipnir.

the fallen blood and came hissing out to display their forked tongues. . . . Perseus had planned to take the quickest route across Europe, but Athene forbade this; asking him to consider the damage he would do if he passed over cities and cultivated lands. On seeing such a large object flying aloft, everyone would look up, and be turned to stone; the corn would also be ruined. So he wheeled about and with the West Wind behind him sailed across Libya, because that was an untilled region, viewed only by the Sun and the stars. . . . Thus, though the Libyan soil was sterile and the fields unproductive, they drank the poisonous blood, dripping from Medusa's head, which became more poisonous still by contact with the loose burning earth. The first snake to spring from the ground after this rain of Gorgon's blood was the deadly asp with its puffed neck; and since the blood happened to be particularly abundant at this point, and mixed with clotted venom, it proved to be the most deadly of all the Libyan varieties. . . .

Among other snakes [is] the Basilisk, which scares away all lesser snakes by its terrifying hiss, and reigns alone over the empty desert—for it can kill without biting.

The Basilisk lives in the desert, then; or rather, it created the desert. Birds fall dead at its feet, and fruits rot; the water in the rivers from which it slakes its thirst is poisoned for hundreds of years. That its glance breaks stones and singes grass has been attested by Pliny. The "effluvium of the weasel is fatal to it," Pliny says; in the Middle Ages people believed that a cock's crowing could kill it, and experienced travelers carried cocks with them when they were about to pass through unknown regions. Another weapon was the mirror: the Basilisk is struck dead by its own image.

Christian encyclopedists rejected the fabulous mythologies of the *Pharsalia* and sought a rational explanation for the Basilisk's origin. (They were obliged to believe in the creature, since the Vulgate translates as "Basilisk" the Hebrew word *Tsepha*, which is the name of a poisonous reptile.) The hypothesis that gained the greatest support was that of a deformed and misshapen egg laid by a cock and brooded upon by a serpent or a toad. In the seventeenth century, Sir Thomas Browne declared that hypothesis to be as monstrous as the creature itself. At more or less the same time, Quevedo wrote his romance *El Basilisco*, where we may read:

> *Si está vivo quien te vió,*
> *Toda su historia es mentira,*
> *Pues si no murió, te ignora,*
> *Y si murió no lo afirma.*

We might translate his lines in this way:

> If alive he is, who one time saw thee,
> The story he tells of thee is lies,
> For if died he not, he never saw thee,
> And if see thee he truly did, he died.

The Behemoth

Four hundred years before the Christian era, Behemoth was a magnification of the elephant or the hippopotamus, or an erroneous and frightened version of those two animals; now, it is neither more nor less than those ten famous Biblical verses that describe the creature (Job 40:15–24) and the vast form that they evoke. The rest is exegesis, or philology.

The name "Behemoth" is actually plural; it is (the philologists tell us) the intensive plural of the Hebrew word *b'hemah*, which simply means "beast." As Fray Luis de León said in his *Exposición del Libro de Job:* "*Behemoth* is a Hebrew word, and is as though saying *beasts;* in the common judgment of the learned, it signifies the elephant, and is thus called for its immense size, for though it be but one animal it is like unto many."

For the sake of the coincidence we might point out that the name of God, *Elohim*, which appears in the first verse of the Bible, is also a plural, though the verb it governs is in the singular ("In the beginning the Gods made [*sing.*] the heavens and the earth") and that this locution has been called the plural of plenitude.*

These are the verses from the King James version of the Bible by which we know the Behemoth:

15 Behold now behemoth, which I made with thee; he eateth grass as an ox.

---

*Analogously, we sometimes find that the first-person plural pronoun "we" is used by persons of great dignity to refer to themselves in speaking; one recalls the famous statement by Queen Victoria: "We are not amused." This is called the "royal plural" or the "royal we." Latterly, nurses also use a similar locution, though in place of the second-person singular.

16 Lo now, his strength is in his loins, and his force is in the navel of his belly.

17 He moveth his tail like a cedar: the sinews of his stones are wrapped together.

18 His bones are as strong pieces of brass; his bones are like bars of iron.

19 He is the chief of the ways of God: he that made him can make his sword to approach unto him.

20 Surely the mountains bring him forth food, where all the beasts of the field play.

21 He lieth under the shady trees, in the covert of the reed, and fens.

22 The shady trees cover him with their shadow; the willows of the brook compass him about.

23 Behold, he drinketh up a river, and hasteth not: he trusteth that he can draw up Jordan into his mouth.

24 He taketh it with his eyes: his nose pierceth through snares.

This, in vaguely different words, is the Douay version:

15 See, besides you I made Behemoth, that feeds on grass like an ox. 16. Behold the strength in his loins, and his vigor in the sinews of his belly. 17. He carries his tail like a cedar; the sinews of his thighs are like cables. 18. His bones are like tubes of bronze; his frame is like iron rods.

19 He came at the beginning of God's ways, and was made the taskmaster of his fellows; 20. for the produce of the mountains is brought to him, and of all wild animals he makes sport.

21 Under the lotus trees he lies, in coverts of the reedy swamp. 22. The lotus trees cover him with their shade; all about

him are the poplars on the bank. 23. If the river grows violent, he is not disturbed; he is tranquil though the torrent surges about his mouth.

The translators of this version feel that the twenty-fourth verse is corrupt in the original, and so end their portrait here.

The Bird That Makes the Rain

In addition to the Dragon, Chinese farmers might call upon the bird known as the Shang Yang to bring them rain. It had but a single leg; in ancient times children would hop on one leg, wrinkle their foreheads, and shout, "It will soon rain, for Shang Yang is frolicking in the yard!" It was said that the bird drank water from the rivers and dropped it upon the land.

In ancient times, a wise man domesticated this fowl, and he would walk about with it upon his sleeve. Historians say that one day the Shang Yang, flapping its wings and hopping on its one leg, passed before the throne of Prince Ch'i, who, alarmed, sent one of his ministers to the court of Lu, to consult with Confucius about this event. Confucius predicted that the Shang Yang would cause floods in the principality and in the lands nearby, and he advised that dikes and canals be built. The prince followed Confucius' advice, and thereby avoided great disasters.

The Borametz

This "vegetable Lamb of Tartary," as Sir Thomas Browne called it in the third book of his *Pseudodoxia Epidemica* (London, 1646), is also known as the Borametz, the *Polypodium borametz*, and the Chinese polypodium. It is a plant shaped like a lamb, covered with golden fleece. It rises from four or five roots, and it "affordeth a bloudy juice upon breaking, and liveth while the plants be consumed about it." "Wolves delight to feed on it," says Browne (probably for the shape of it, he adds).

In other monsters, species or genuses of animals are combined; in the Borametz, it is the animal and vegetable kingdoms.

We might recall another such case, that of the Mandrake, or Mandragora, which screams like a man when it is pulled from the ground; there is also, in one of the circles of Hell, that sad forest of suicides from whose "broken splints come words and blood at once," and that tree dreamed by Chesterton, which devoured the birds that nested in its branches and which put out feathers instead of leaves when springtime came.

The Brownies

These are helpful little brown men whose name is derived from their color. They visit farms in Scotland while the family is asleep and lend a hand with the household's chores. One of the Grimms' stories tells of a similar occurrence.

The famed author Robert Louis Stevenson declared that he'd trained his Brownies to be writers. As he slept, they would whisper fantastic plots in his ear—for example, the strange case of Dr. Jekyll and the diabolical Mr. Hyde, and that episode in "Olalla" when a young man from an old Spanish family bites his sister's hand.

Buraq

The first verse of the seventeenth *sura* of the Qur'an reads as follows: "Glory be to Him who carried his servant by night from the sacred temple of Mecca to the temple that is more remote, whose precinct we have blessed, that we might show him of our signs!" Commentators tell us that the praised one is God, the servant is Mohammed, the sacred temple that of Mecca, the distant temple that of Jerusalem; we are also informed that from Jerusalem the Prophet was transported to the

seventh heaven. In the most ancient versions of the legend, Mohammed was guided by a man or an angel; in those of a later date, he is taken by a celestial steed, larger than an ass and smaller than a mule. This animal is Buraq, or Borak, whose name means "the shining (or resplendent) one." Captain Burton tells us that the Muslims of India generally portray Buraq with the head of a man, the ears of an ass, the body of a horse, and the wings and tail of a peacock.

One Islamic *hadith* tells us that as Buraq flew upward from the earth it kicked over a jar filled with water. The Prophet was taken up to the seventh heaven, where he spoke with each of the patriarchs and angels that reside there, crossed the Oneness, and felt a chill that froze his heart when the hand of God patted him on the shoulder. The time of men is not the time of God; when he returned to earth, the Prophet caught the jar before a single drop of water had spilled out of it.

Miguel Asín Palacios reminds us of a Murcian mystic who lived in the thirteenth century and wrote an allegory titled "The Book of the Night Journey to the Majesty of the Most Generous One." In this volume, the author made Buraq symbolize Divine Love. In another text, we read that Buraq may be compared with "purity of intention."

The Cheshire Cat and Kilkenny Cats

E veryone has heard the expression "to grin like a Cheshire cat." Several explanations for this saying have been proposed. One is that cheese in the shape of a laughing cat was sold in Cheshire. Another would have it that Cheshire was made an earldom, and that this provoked the hilarity of the county's cats. Still another claims that in the times of Richard III there was a sheriff, one Caterling, who smiled ferociously when he caught poachers at their work.

In the dreamlike novel *Alice in Wonderland,* published in 1865, Lewis Carroll gave the Cheshire Cat the ability to disappear gradually, until only its smile was left.

It is said of the Kilkenny Cats that they got into furious fights and devoured each other, leaving only their tails. This story dates from the eighteenth century.

The Catoblepas

Pliny (VIII, 32) recounts that within the borders of Ethiopia, not far from the sources of the Nile, one finds the Catoblepas:

An animal of moderate size, and in other respects sluggish in the movement of the rest of its limbs; its head is remarkably heavy, and it only carries it with the greatest difficulty, being always bent down towards the earth. Were it not for this circumstance, it would prove the destruction of the human race; for all who behold its eyes, fall dead upon the spot.

In Greek, "Catoblepas" means "to look downward." Cuvier has suggested that the antelope gnu (contaminated by the Basilisk and the Gorgons) was the Ancients' inspiration for the Catoblepas. Toward the end of *The Temptation of St. Anthony*, we read the following words:

THE CATOBLEPAS

(*A black buffalo with a pig's head, falling to the ground, and attached to his shoulders by a neck long, thin, and flaccid as an empty gut.*

He wallows flat upon the ground, and his feet entirely disappear beneath the enormous mane of coarse hair which covers his face):

"Fat, melancholy, fierce thus I continually remain, feeling against my belly the warmth of the mud. So heavy is my skull that it is impossible for me to lift it. I roll it slowly all around me, open-mouthed; and with my tongue I tear up the venomous plants bedewed with my breath. Once, I even devoured my own feet without knowing it!

"No one, Anthony, has ever beheld mine eyes, or at least, those who have beheld them are dead. Were I to lift my eyelids—my pink and swollen eyelids—thou wouldst forthwith die!"

The Centaur

The Centaur is the most harmonious creature in fantastic zoology. In the *Metamorphoses*, Ovid calls it "biform," but it is easy enough to overlook its heterogeneous nature and to think that in the Platonic world of essences there is an archetype of the Centaur just as there is of the Horse or of Man. The discovery of that archetype took many centuries; primitive and archaic monuments portray a nude man to which a horse's rump can only uncomfortably be fitted. On the western facade of the Temple of Zeus on Olympia, the Centaurs have equine limbs; at the place from which the animal's neck should emerge, there emerges the torso of a man.

Ixion, the king of Thessaly, was said to have engendered the race of Centaurs upon a cloud to whom Zeus gave the shape of Hera; another legend has it that they are the children of Apollo. (It has been said that the word "Centaur" derives from "gandharva"; in Vedic mythology, the Gandharva are minor deities who rule over the horses of the sun.) Since the Greeks of Homer's time did not ride horses, it is conjectured that the first nomad they saw seemed to them to be one with his steed, and it is also alleged that the Indians of the New World saw Pizarro's and Hernán Cortés' soldiers as Centaurs. William H. Prescott's *History of the Conquest of Peru* gives the following account of that first meeting:

> It might have gone hard with the Spaniards, hotly pressed by their resolute enemy so superior in numbers, but for a ludicrous accident reported by the historians as happening to one of the cavaliers. This was a fall from his horse,

which so astonished the barbarians, who were not prepared for this division of what seemed one and the same being into two, that, filled with consternation, they fell back, and left a way open for the Christians to regain their vessels!

But unlike the Indians of the New World, the Greeks did know the horse. It seems more likely that the Centaur was a deliberately drawn image, not some ignorant confusion.

The most popular of the fables in which the Centaurs figure is that of their battle with the Lapiths, who had invited them to a wedding feast. The guests were unused to wine; in the midst of the celebration, a drunken and lustfully inflamed Centaur, Eurytus, seized the bride and, overturning tables, set in motion the famous Centauromachia that Phidias or one of his followers sculpted on the Parthenon, Ovid sang in the twelfth book of the *Metamorphoses*, and Rubens took for inspiration. The Centaurs, defeated by the Lapiths, had to flee to Thessaly. In another battle, Hercules' arrows extinguished the entire race.

Anger and rustic barbarism are symbolized in the Centaur, though Achilles and Æsculapius were tutored by Chiron, "the most gentlemanly" of the Centaurs (*Iliad*, Book XI), who instructed his charges in the arts of music, hunting, warfare, and even medicine and surgery. Chiron figures memorably in the twelfth canto of Dante's *Inferno*, which is generally called the "Centaur canto." See, in this regard, the fine observations made by Momigliano, in his 1945 edition.

Pliny says that he saw a Hippocentaur, preserved in honey, which was sent to the emperor from Egypt.

In his *Dinner of the Seven Wise Men*, Plutarch tells the humorous story of one of the youths who tended the flocks of Periander, despot of Corinth. It seems the herdsman brought the ruler the foal, wrapped in a leather bag, that a certain mare had given birth to just that morning; the newborn's face, neck, and arms were human, while the rest of its body was that of a horse. It cried like a baby, and everyone thought this a terrifying omen. The wise Thales looked at it, however, laughed, and told Periander that he should either not employ such young men as keepers of his horses or provide wives for them.

In the fifth book of his poem *De Rerum Natura*, Lucretius declares the Centaur an impossible creature:

> Centaurs never existed, nor at any time can there be creatures of double nature and twofold body combined together of incompatible limbs, such that the powers of the two halves can be fairly balanced. Here is a proof that will convince the dullest wit.
>
> Firstly, the horse is at the best of his vigour when three years have passed round; not so the boy by any means, for even at this time he will often in sleep seek his mother's milky breast. Afterwards, when the strong powers of the horse are failing in old age and his body faints as life recedes, then is the time of the flower of boyhood, when youth is beginning and is clothing the cheeks with soft down.

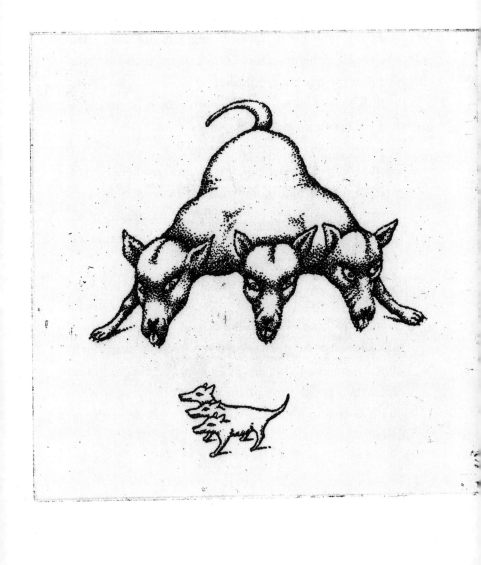

Cerberus

I f the Inferno is a house, the house of Hades, it is only natural that it should have a dog to guard it; it is only natural, too, that the dog be imagined as terrifying. Hesiod's *Theogony* gives Cerberus fifty heads; for the greater convenience of the plastic arts, this number has been reduced, and now it is common knowledge that Cerberus has *three* heads. Virgil mentions the creature's three gullets; Ovid, its triple bark; Butler compares the three crowns of the diadem worn by the Pope, who is Heaven's doorman, with the three heads of the dog who stands at the gates of Hell. Dante gives the creature certain human characteristics that make its hellishness even more terrible: "his eyeballs glare a bloodshot crimson, and his bearded jowls are greasy and black; pot-bellied, talon-heeled, he clutches and flays and rips and rends the souls. They howl in the rain like hounds." The beast bites, barks, and shows its fangs "a-gloat."

Bringing Cerberus out into the light of day was the last of the labors of Hercules. An eighteenth-century writer, one Zachary Grey, interprets this adventure in this way:

> This Dog with three Heads denotes the paſt, the preſent, and the Time to come; which receive, and, as it were, devour all things. *Hercules* got the better of him, which ſhews that heroick Actions are always victorious over Time, becauſe they are preſent in the Memory of Poſterity.

According to the most ancient texts, those who enter Hell are greeted by Cerberus with its tail (which is a serpent), while the creature's three heads devour those who try to leave. A later tradition has it bite those who *arrive;* in order to pacify the beast, it was customary to put a honey cake into the dead man's casket.

In Scandinavian mythology, a bloody dog named Garmr guards the house of the dead and will battle the gods when the wolves of hell devour the moon and the sun. Some give this dog four eyes; the dogs of Yama, the Brahmin god of death, also have four eyes.

Brahmanism and Buddhism offer hells filled with dogs which, like the Dantean Cerberus, are torturers of the souls of the dead.

The Chimæra

The first mention of the Chimæra is in the sixth book of *The Iliad*. There, we read that the creature was of divine descent and that "her forepart [was] lionish, her tail a snake's, a she-goat in between"; she "exhaled in jets a rolling fire" and was at last killed by the handsome Bellerophontes, son of Glaucus, as the gods had foretold. The head of a lion, belly of a she-goat, and tail of a serpent is the most natural interpretation admitted by Homer's words, but Hesiod, in his *Theogony*, describes the Chimæra as follows:

> Her heads were three: one was that of a glare-eyed lion,
> one of a goat, and the third of a snake, a powerful dragon.

The creature is portrayed in Arezzo's famous bronze, which dates from the fifth century, as Hesiod describes her (for all concede that the beast is female); the goat's head is in the middle of her back, while the lion's and serpent's are at the creature's two extremes.

In the sixth book of the *Æneid* the Chimæra appears again, "breathing dangerous flames"; the commentator Servius Honoratus has observed that all authorities agree that the monster came originally from Lycia, where there is a volcano that bears its name. The base of the volcano is infested with serpents; on its sides there are meadows where goats pasture; and on the top, flames shoot forth and lions have their dens. The Chimæra might, then, be a metaphor for that wonderful mountain. Earlier, Plutarch had suggested that "ChimÆra" was the name of a ship's captain with tendencies toward the piratical; he had painted a lion, a she-goat, and a snake on his ship.

These absurd conjectures prove that people were already growing a bit tired of the Chimæra. It was better to translate the beast into something (anything) else than to picture it as it was. It was too heterogeneous; the lion, the she-goat, and the serpent (in some texts, the dragon) resisted merging into a single animal. In time, the fearsome Chimæra became "chimerical"; a famous quip by Rabelais (who asked whether a Chimæra, bobbing about in the void, would eat puns) is perhaps the watershed. The incoherent shape fades away and the word remains, to stand for "the Impossible." "An illusion or fabrication of the mind" is the definition one finds in the dictionary today.

The Celestial Cock

The Chinese believe that the Celestial Cock is a bird with golden feathers that crows three times each day: first, when the sun takes its morning bath in the ocean; second, when the sun is at its zenith; and last, when the sun sinks into the west. The first cock-crow shakes the skies and wakes all humanity. The Celestial Cock is an ancestor of Yang, the masculine principle in the universe. It has three legs and builds its nest in the Fu-sang tree, whose height is measured in hundreds of miles and which grows in the region of the dawn. The voice of the Celestial Cock is strong, and its bearing is majestic. It lays eggs from which hatch red-combed chicks that answer the Celestial Cock's crowing every morning. All the cocks of the earth descend from the Celestial Cock, which is also known as the Bird of Dawn.

The Crocotta and the Leucrocotta

Ctesias, physician to Artaxerxes Mnemon, employed Persian sources for his portrayal of India, a work titled the *Indica*; this book is of incalculable value for the light it throws on the way in which the Persians of Artaxerxes' time imagined that other land. Chapter XXXII of Ctesias' anthology gives a report of the Cynolycus, or "dog-wolf"; Pliny (VIII, 30) gave that hypothetical animal the name Crocotta, and said that "it can break any thing with its teeth, and instantly on swallowing it digest it with the stomach."

More precise than the description of the Crocotta is that of the Leucrotta, or Leucrocotta, in which some commentators have seen reflections of the gnu, others of the hyena, and others, a fusion of the two. It is, says Pliny, "a wild beast of extraordinary swiftness, the size of the wild ass, with the legs of a stag, the neck, tail, and breast of a lion, the head of a badger, a cloven hoof, the mouth slit up as far as the ears, and one continuous bone instead of teeth." This animal lived in Ethiopia (where there are also wild bulls armed with movable horns) and it is said that it could sweetly imitate the human voice.

A Crossbreed by Kafka

I have a curious animal, half-cat, half-lamb. It is a legacy from my father. But it only developed in my time; formerly it was far more lamb than cat. Now it is both in about equal parts. From the cat it takes its head and claws, from the lamb its size and shape; from both its eyes, which are wild and changing, its hair, which is soft, lying close to its body, its movements, which partake both of skipping and slinking. Lying on the window-sill in the sun it curls itself up in a ball and purrs; out in the meadow it rushes about as if mad and is scarcely to be caught. It flies from cats and makes to attack lambs. On moonlight nights its favourite promenade is the tiles. It cannot mew and it loathes rats. Beside the hen-coop it can lie for hours in ambush, but it has never yet seized an opportunity for murder.

I feed it on milk; that seems to suit it best. In long draughts it sucks the milk into it through its teeth of a beast of prey. Naturally it is a great source of entertainment for children. Sunday morning is the visiting hour. I sit with the little beast on my knees, and the children of the whole neighbourhood stand round me.

Then the strangest questions are asked, which no human being could answer: Why there is only one such animal, why I rather than anybody else should own it, whether there was ever an animal like it before and what would happen if it died, whether it feels lonely, why it has no children, what it is called, etc.

I never trouble to answer, but confine myself without further explanation to exhibiting my possession. Sometimes the children bring cats with them; once they actually brought two lambs. But against all their hopes there was no scene of recognition. The animals gazed calmly at each other with their animal eyes, and obviously accepted their reciprocal existence as a divine fact.

Sitting on my knees the beast knows neither fear nor lust of pursuit. Pressed against me it is happiest. It remains faithful to the family that brought it up. In that there is certainly no extraordinary mark of fidelity, but merely the true instinct of an animal which, though it has countless step-relations in the world, has perhaps not a single blood relation, and to which consequently the protection it has found with us is sacred.

Sometimes I cannot help laughing when it sniffs round me and winds itself between my legs and simply will not be parted from me. Not content with being lamb and cat, it almost insists on being a dog as well. Once when, as may happen to any one, I could see no way out of my business difficulties and all that depends on such things, and had resolved to let everything go, and in this mood was lying in my rocking-chair in my room, the beast on my knees, I happened to glance down and saw tears dropping from its huge whiskers. Were they mine, or were they the animal's? Had this cat, along with the soul of a lamb, the ambitions of a human being? I did not inherit much from my father, but this legacy is worth looking at.

It has the restlessness of both beasts, that of the cat and that of the lamb, diverse as they are. For that reason its skin feels too narrow for it. Sometimes it jumps up on the armchair beside me, plants its front legs on my shoulder, and puts its muzzle to my ear. It is as if it were saying something to me, and as a matter of fact it turns its head afterwards and gazes in my face to see the impression its communication has made. And to oblige it I behave as if I had understood and nod. Then it jumps to the floor and dances about with joy.

Perhaps the knife of the butcher would be a release for this animal; but as it is a legacy I must deny it that. So it must wait until the breath voluntarily leaves its body, even though it sometimes gazes at me with a look of human understanding, challenging me to do the thing of which both of us are thinking.

—Franz Kafka

The Demons of Judaism

L ying between the world of flesh and the world of the spirit, Judaic superstition has it, there is an orb inhabited by angels and demons. Its population exceeds all arithmetical possibility. Through the centuries, Egypt, Babylonia, and Persia have helped shape this fantastic world. Perhaps under the influence of Christianity (Trachtenberg suggests), Demonology, or the science of demons, came to be less important than Angelology, or the science of angels.

We might, however, mention the name Keteh Meriri, the Lord of Midday and Hot Summers. A group of children on their way to school met up with him; all but two of them died. During the thirteenth century Judaic Demonology was infiltrated by Latin, French, and German interlopers, who began to commingle with those listed in the Talmud.

Swedenborg's Demons

The Demons of Emanuel Swedenborg (1688–1772) are not a species apart; they belong to the species of mankind. They are individuals who, after death, choose Hell. They are not happy in that region of marshes, deserts, jungles, fire-ravaged villages, brothels, and dark lairs, but they would be unhappier still in Heaven. Sometimes a ray of celestial light penetrates to where they are; the Demons experience it as a fiery burning and a foul stench. They consider themselves beautiful, but many of them have faces like beasts, or mere pieces of flesh, or have no faces at all. They live in mutual hatred and armed violence; if they come together, they do so in order to destroy one another or someone else. God forbids men and angels to draw a map of Hell, but we know that its general shape is that of a Demon. The most sordid and horrible hells are in the west.

The Devourer of the Dead

There is a curious literary genre that has arisen independently in many ages and nations: the guide for the dead through the underworld. Swedenborg's *Heaven and Hell*, gnostic writings, the Tibetan *Book of the Dead* (the *Bardo Thödol*, a title which should, according to W. Y. Evans-Wentz, be translated rather as "Liberation Through Hearing on the After-Death Plane"), and the Egyptian *Book of the Dead* are but some of the possible examples. The similarities and differences of the two last-named books have merited the close attention of scholars; here, we will merely repeat the observation that in the Tibetan work the other world is as illusory as this one, while for the Egyptians the other world is real and objective.

In both texts there is a tribunal of deities, some with monkey heads; in both, there is a weighing of good deeds against bad. In the Egyptian *Book of the Dead*, the deceased person's heart is weighed against a feather on the two disks of the scales; in the *Bardo Thödol*, small white stones are weighed against a pile of black. For the Tibetans, demons act as the furious torturers of those who are found wanting; for the Egyptians, it is Ammit, the Devourer of Souls.

The dead Egyptian stands before the tribunal and the balance scale and makes his declaration: he swears he has not made hungry, swears he has not made to weep, swears he has not killed or commanded to kill, swears he has not destroyed the loaves of the gods or taken away the food of the spirits, swears he has not falsified weights, swears he has not taken the milk from the mouths of children, swears he has not deprived the herds of their pastures, swears he has not trapped birds in the preserves of the gods.

If he lies, the forty-two judges remand him to Ammit, the Devourer of the Dead, "whose foreparts are a crocodile, whose middle is a lion, and whose hindparts are those of a hippopotamus," and who stands ever ready at the Weighing of the Heart to gobble up the heart weighed down with sin. This creature is aided by another animal, Babai, about which we know only that it is fearsome and that Plutarch identifies it with a Titan, the father of the Chimæra.

The Double

S uggested or inspired by mirrors, the surface of still water, and twins, the concept of the Double is common to many lands. It seems likely that statements such as Pythagoras' "A friend is another myself" and Plato's "Know thyself" were inspired by it. In Germany, it is called the *Doppelgänger*; in Scotland, the *fetch*, because it comes to fetch men to their death. Meeting oneself was, therefore, most ominous; the tragic ballad "Ticonderoga" by Robert Louis Stevenson recounts a legend on this theme. We might also recall that strange painting by Rossetti called "How They Met Themselves"—two lovers meet themselves at dusk in a forest. One need only mention other instances in Hawthorne, Dostoyevsky, and Alfred de Musset.

For the Jews, on the other hand, the apparition of the Double was not a foreshadowing of death, but rather a proof that the person to whom it appeared had achieved the rank of prophet. This is the explanation offered by Gershom Scholem. A tradition included in the Talmud tells the story of a man, searching for God, who met himself.

In Poe's story "William Wilson," the Double is the hero's conscience; when the hero kills his double, he dies. In the poetry of William Butler Yeats, the Double is our "other side," our opposite, our complement, that person that we are not and shall never be.

Plutarch wrote that the Greeks called the king's representative the "other I."

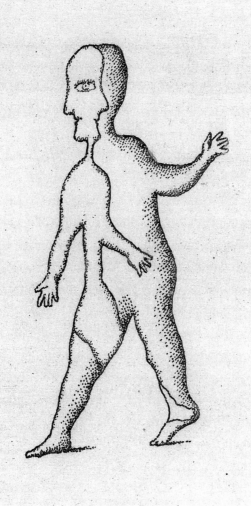

The Dragon

The Dragon possesses the ability to assume diverse, though inscrutable, forms. It is a creature generally imagined with the head of a horse, the tail of a serpent, large wings on each side of its body, and four claws, each with four great talons. Legend tells also of its nine resemblances: its horns resemble those of a stag; its head, that of a camel; its eyes, those of a demon; its throat, that of a serpent; its belly, that of a mollusk; its scales, those of a fish; its claws, those of the eagle; the pads of its feet, those of the tiger; and its ears, those of the ox. There are examples of earless Dragons that hear through their horns. They are customarily portrayed with a pearl hung about their necks—the emblem of the sun. It is in that pearl that their power resides; they are harmless if it can be taken away from them.

History traces the first emperors to the race of Dragons. The creature's bones, teeth, and saliva possess medicinal virtues. It can, if it wishes, be visible to men or invisible. In springtime it rises into the heavens; in the fall, it sinks into the depths of the oceans. Some Dragons have no wings, and fly as if by magic. Science, Willoughby-Meade tells us, distinguishes several varieties, to wit: "The Celestial Dragon, which supports and guards the mansions of the gods; the Spiritual Dragon, which causes the wind to blow and the beneficent rain to water the ground; the Earth Dragon, who marks out the courses of rivers and streams; the Dragon of Hidden Treasure, in charge of the metals and precious stones buried in the earth." Buddhists say that there are as many Dragons as the fish in their many concentric seas; somewhere in the universe, there exists a sacred cipher that expresses their exact number. The people of China believe in Dragons more than in other deities because they see Dragons so often in the changing clouds. Thus it was that Shakespeare observed that "sometimes we see a cloud that's dragonish."

The Dragon rules mountains, is linked to geomancy, lives near tombs, is associated with the cult of Confucius, is the Neptune of the seas, and appears on dry land. The kings of the Sea Dragons live in shining palaces under water and their sustenance is pearls and opals. There are five of these kings: the greatest is in the center, and the other four correspond to the four points of the compass. Each one is a league in length; the wriggling of their bodies makes the mountains crash together. Their bodies are armored with yellow scales. Their chins are bearded and their legs and tails are hairy. Their brows hang over their gleaming eyes, their ears are small but thick, their mouths are always open, their tongues are long and their teeth sharp. Their very breath boils the fishes of the sea, and the exhalations of their bodies roast them. When these Dragons rise to the surface of the oceans, whirlpools and typhoons result; when they fly through the air, they cause storms that tear the roofs off houses in the cities and flood the countryside. They are immortal and can communicate wordlessly with each other in spite of the distances that separate them. In the third month of each year they make a report to their superior deities.

The Chinese Dragon

Chinese cosmogony teaches that the Ten Thousand Beings (the world) were born from the rhythmic oscillation of the two complementary eternal principles Yin and Yang. Yin is linked to concentration, darkness, passivity, even numbers, and cold; Yang, to growth, light, vigor, odd numbers, and heat. The female, the Earth, the color orange, valleys, riverbeds, and the tiger are symbols of Yin, while Yang is symbolized by the male, the sky, the color blue, mountains, pillars, and the Dragon.

Lung, the Chinese Dragon, is one of the four magical animals; the others are the Unicorn, the Phoenix, and the Turtle. The Dragon of the Western world is terrifying in the best of cases, ridiculous in the worst; the *Lung* of Chinese tradition possesses divinity and is like an angel that is also a lion. Thus we read in Ssu-Ma Ch'ien's *Records of the Historian* that Confucius went one day to visit the archivist (or librarian) Lao Tse, and after his visit said:

> "Birds fly, fish swim, and animals run. Whatever runs may be stopped by a trap; whatever swims may be caught by a net; whatever flies may be stopped by an arrow. But then there is the Dragon; I do not know how it gallops on the wind or how it rises into the sky. Today, I have seen Lao Tse and I can say that I have seen the Dragon."

A Dragon, or a Dragon-Horse, rose out of the Yellow River and revealed to the emperor the famous circular diagram that symbolizes the reciprocal play of Yin and Yang; the stables of a certain king housed Dragons for riding and Dragons suited for drawing carriages; another king ate the flesh of Dragons and his kingdom prospered. A great poet, to illustrate the dangers of high position, wrote: "The Unicorn winds up cold meat, the Dragon a meat pie."

In the *I Ching* (*The Book of Changes*), the Dragon often symbolizes the wise man.

For hundreds of years the Dragon was the symbol of the Empire. The Emperor's throne was called the Dragon Throne, his face, the Dragon Visage. The phrase used to announce that the emperor had died was "he has ascended into the heavens on a Dragon."

Popular imagination links the Dragon to clouds, to the rain that farmers yearn for, and to great rivers. "The earth mates with the Dragon" is a way of saying "rain." In the sixth century, Chang Seng-Yu painted a mural in which there were four Dragons. Those who saw the painting criticized him because he had left out the Dragons' eyes. Chang was angered by this, and so he once more took up his brushes and completed two of the four sinuous figures. At that, "the air filled with thunder and lightning, the wall split asunder, and the Dragons ascended into the sky. But the other two Dragons, those without eyes, remained where they had been painted."

The Chinese Dragon has horns, claws, and scales; along its spine there is a sort of saw-toothed ridge. It is customarily portrayed with a pearl hung about its neck—the emblem of the sun. In that pearl lies its power; it is harmless if the pearl can be taken away from it.

Chang Tzu tells us of a persevering man who after three laborious years mastered the art of dragon-slaying. For the rest of his days, he had not a single opportunity to test his skills.

The Western Dragon

A tall, lumbering serpent with claws and wings is, perhaps, the most faithful description of the Dragon. It may be black, but it must also gleam; likewise, its mouth is required to breathe out fire and smoke. This, of course, is its present-day portrayal; the Greeks seem to have given the name "Dragon" to any large serpent. Pliny tells us that in the summer, Dragons crave the blood of elephants, which is remarkably cold. The Dragon flings itself upon the Elephant, coils about it, and sinks its teeth into its throat; the Elephant, bled by the Dragon, falls to the ground and dies, but the Dragon dies as well, under the weight of its adversary. We also read in Pliny that the Dragons of Ethiopia often cross the Red Sea into Arabia, in search of better sources of nourishment. In order to perform this feat, four or five Dragons "twist and interlace together like so many osiers in a hurdle." Another chapter is devoted to the remedies derived from the Dragon; there, we read that a Dragon's "eyes, dried and beaten up with honey, form a liniment which is an effectual preservative against the terrors of spectres by night," and, somewhat more skeptically, that "the fat adhering to the heart, attached to the arm with a deer's sinews in the skin of a gazelle, will ensure success in law-suits, it is said." Likewise, the Dragon's "teeth, attached to the body with a deer's sinews in the skin of a roe-buck, have the effect of rendering masters indulgent and potentates gracious, it is said." The text even more doubtfully mentions a preparation by which "lying magicians profess to render persons invincible. They take the tail and head of a dragon, the hairs of a lion's forehead with the marrow of that animal, the foam of a horse that has won a race, and the claws of a dog's feet:

these they tie up together in a deer's skin, and fasten them alternately with the sinews of a deer and a gazelle."

In the eleventh book of *The Iliad*, we read that the shield of Agamemnon was emblazoned with a blue, three-headed Dragon; hundreds of years later, Scandinavian pirates painted Dragons on their shields and carved Dragons' heads on the prows of their ships. Among the Romans, the Dragon was the symbol of the cohort as the Eagle was the insignia of the legion; that is the origin of the present-day "dragoons." There were Dragons on the banners and pennants of the Germanic kings of England. The object of these images was to plant terror in the hearts of their enemies. Thus, in the ballad of Athis we read:

> *Ce souloient Romains porter.*
> *Ce nous fait moult à redouter.*

> This which the Romans used to bear
> Makes ourselves be greatly feared.

In the West, the Dragon was always thought of as evil. One of the classic feats or labors of the hero (Hercules, Sigurd, St. Michael, St. George) was to defeat and slay a Dragon. In Germanic legends, the Dragon guarded precious objects; thus, in *Beowulf,* composed in eighth-century England, there is a Dragon that guards a hoard of treasure for three hundred years. An escaped slave hides in the Dragon's cave and steals a goblet, or a chalice. The Dragon (called "the Worm") wakes up, discovers the theft, and resolves to kill the robber; every once in a while he goes down into the cave and searches to be sure the goblet has not simply been mislaid. (A brilliant idea on the part of the poet, giving such human uncertainty to the monster.) The Dragon begins to "vomit flames" and lay waste to the kingdom; Beowulf goes out to find the Dragon, battles it, and slays it.

People really believed in Dragons. This is attested to even as late as the mid–sixteenth century, in Konrad von Gesner's *Historia Animalium*, a scientific treatise.

Time has considerably tarnished the prestige of Dragons. We believe in lions as reality and as symbol; we believe in the Minotaur as symbol, though no longer as reality; the Dragon is perhaps the best known though also the least fortunate of fantastic animals. It strikes us as puerile, a creature of childhood, and its puerility contaminates the stories in which it figures. But we must not forget that this is a modern prejudice, perhaps inspired by the excess of Dragons found in fairy tales. In Revelations, the Dragon is named four separate times: "the dragon, that old serpent, which is the Devil, and Satan" (Revelations 20:2). Analogously, St. Augustine writes *"Diabolus draco dicitur propter insidias, quia occulte insidiatur,"* or as Gesner translates, "the deuill is called a dragon becaufe of his treachery, for he doth treacherously fet vpon men to deftroy them." Jung observes that the Dragon combines the serpent and the bird, the elements of earth and air.

The Elephant That Prefigured the Birth of Buddha

Five centuries before the Christian era, Queen Maya, in Nepal, dreamed that a white elephant, who came down from the Mountain of God, entered into her body. This oneiric animal had six tusks, which symbolized the six dimensions of Hindustani space: up, down, behind, before, left, and right. The king's astrologers predicted that Maya would give birth to a child who would be Emperor of the Earth or Redeemer of All Humanity. It was the second of these predictions, as we know, that came to pass.

In India, the elephant is a domestic animal. The color white symbolizes humility, and the number six is sacred.

The Eloi and the Morlocks

In *The Time Machine,* the novel published by a young H. G. Wells in 1895, a mechanical device enables the hero to travel into a far distant future. There he discovers that the genus *Homo* has divided into two species: the Eloi—delicate, defenseless aristocrats who dwell in idle gardens and live on fruit, and the Morlocks—a subterranean race of workers, proletarians, who have become blind from working in the darkness. These Morlocks, creatures of routine, continue to run complex, though rusty, machinery which manufactures nothing. Holes in the earth fitted with spiral staircases connect the two worlds. On moonless nights the Morlocks swarm out of their imprisonment and devour the Eloi.

The hero manages to escape back to the present. The only trophy he brings with him is an unknown, withered flower which turns to dust in the here and now, but which someday, thousands of centuries from now, will bloom.

Elves

Elves are of Germanic descent. We know very little about their appearance, except that they are sinister looking and tiny. They steal livestock and also children, and they delight in mischief and deviltry. In England the name "elf-lock" is given tangled hair, because it is "like the work of the Little 'Uns." There was an Anglo-Saxon spell to counteract the Elves' malevolent ability to shoot tiny arrows from a distance, which, penetrating the skin without leaving a mark, caused neuralgic aches and pains. In German, "nightmare" translates *Alp*, and etymologists derive this word from "elf," since in the Middle Ages there was a widespread belief that Elves would press down upon the sleeper's chest and cause frightful dreams.

Fairies

The name of these creatures is linked to the Latin word *fatum*, meaning "fate" or "destiny"; with their magic they intervene in the affairs of men. Some have said that the Fairies are the most numerous, beautiful, and memorable of the minor deities. They are not limited to any one region or time; the ancient Greeks, the Eskimos, and the American Indians tell stories of heroes who have won the love of these fantastic creatures. Such adventures are dangerous, however: once the Fairy's passion is satisfied, it may kill its lover.

In Ireland and Scotland, Fairies are said to have underground dwellings where they lock up the men, women, and children

that they kidnap. People believe that the neolithic arrowheads they dig up in their fields once belonged to the Fairies, and that these arrowheads possess unfailing medicinal properties.

Fairies like singing and music and the color green. In the late seventeenth century, a Scottish cleric, one Reverend Kirk, of Aberfoyle, compiled a treatise titled *The Secret Commonwealth of the Elves, Fairies, and Fauns.* In 1815, Sir Walter Scott had Kirk's manuscript printed. Mr. Kirk was said to have been carried off by the Fairies because he had revealed their secrets. In the seas off Italy, there is a Fairy, the Fata Morgana, that weaves mirages that confuse sailors and make them lose their course.

The Fastitocalon

The Middle Ages believed that the Holy Spirit had composed two books. The first, as we all know, was the Bible; the second, the Universe, whose creatures contain immortal teachings. To explain the lessons contained in this second book, bestiaries were compiled. In one Anglo-Saxon bestiary we find the following text, translated here into modern English:

> Now again I sing
> about the fishes' kind;
> . . .
> concerning the great Whale,
> which is unwillingly often met,
> cruel and fierce
> to seafarers,
> to every mortal,
> to which the name is given,
> to the ocean-floater,
> Fastitocalon.
> Like is its aspect
> to a rough stone,
> it, as it were, roves
> by the sea-shore,
> by sand-hills surrounded,
> of sea-aits [islands] greatest
> so that imagine
> wavefarers
> that on some island they
> gaze with their eyes,

and then fasten
their high-prow'd ships
to that false land
with anchor-ropes,
settle their sea-horses
at the sea's end,
and then on to that island
mount,
bold of spirit;
the vessels stand
fast by the shore,
by the stream encircled:
then encamp,
weary in mind,
the seafarers
(they of peril dream not)
on that island;
they waken flame,
a high fire kindle;
the men are joyful,
the sad in spirit
of rest desirous.
When feels the skill'd-in-guile,
that on him voyagers
firmly rest,
habitation hold,
in the weather exulting,
then suddenly
into the salt wave,
with the bark,
down goes
the ocean's guest,

seeks the abyss,
and then, in the hall of death,
to the flood commits
ship with men. . . .

He has another property,
the water-rager proud,
yet more cunning:
when him in the sea
hunger afflicts,
and the wretch
lusts after food,
then the ocean-ward
his mouth opens,
his wide lips,
a pleasant odour comes
from his inside,
so that thereby other
kinds of sea-fishes
are deceiv'd;
eager they swim to
where the sweet odour
cometh out:
they there enter
in heedless shoal,
till that the wide jaw
is filled:
then suddenly
around the prey
together crash
the grim gums. . . .

Hell's latticed doors have not
return or escape,
outlet ever,
for those who enter,
any more than the fishes,
sporting in ocean.

The same fable may be found in the *Book of the Thousand Nights and a Night*, in the legend of St. Brendan, and in Milton's *Paradise Lost*, which gives us the whale "slumbering on the Norway foam."

Fauna of China

The *Chiang-liang* has the head of a tiger, the face of a man, four hooves, long extremities, and a snake between its teeth.

In the region to the west of the Red Water lives the animal called *Ch'ou-t'i*, which has a head on both ends of its body.

The inhabitants of Ch'uan-T'ou have human heads, the wings of a bat, and the beak of a bird. They eat nothing but raw fish.

The *Hsiao* is a bird similar to a hawk, but it has the head of a man, the body of a monkey, and the tail of a dog. Its appearance presages harsh droughts.

The *Hsing-hsing* are animals like monkeys. They have white faces and pointed ears. They walk erect like men, and climb trees.

The *Hsing-t'ien* is a headless creature that fought against the gods and was decapitated; it has remained ever afterward headless. Its eyes are in its breast and its mouth is its navel. It hops and skips through the open countryside, brandishing its axe and its shield.

The *Hua*, a flying serpent-fish, looks like a fish but has the wings of a bird. Its appearance presages drought.

The *Hui*, which lives in the mountains, looks like a dog with the face of a man. It is an excellent jumper, and can run as swiftly as an arrow; for this reason people believe that its appearance presages typhoons. It laughs mockingly when it sees man.

The knuckles of those who live in the Land of the Long Arms touch the ground. They live on fish they catch in traps along the shore of the ocean.

The *Sea Men* have the head and arms of a man, but the body and tail of fish. They emerge at the surface of the Strong Waters.

The *Musical Serpent* has the head of a serpent and four wings. It makes a sound like that of the musical stone.

The *Ping-feng*, which lives in the Land of Magic Water, looks like a black pig, but it has a head on each end of its body.

The *Celestial Horse* looks like a white dog with a black head. It has fleshy wings and can fly.

In the Region of the Singular Arm, people have one arm and three eyes. They are remarkably dexterous, and are able to build flying carriages, on which they travel through the air.

The *Ti-chiang* is a supernatural bird that lives in the Celestial Mountains. It is bright red and has six legs and four wings, but it has neither a face nor eyes.

—T'ai Kuang Chi

Fauna of the United States

The wry mythology of the Wisconsin and Minnesota lumber camps includes remarkable creatures—creatures that no one, surely, has ever believed in.

The *Hide-behind* is always hiding behind something. Whichever way a man turns, it's always behind him, which is why nobody has ever satisfactorily described one, though it has killed and eaten many a lumberjack.

The *Roperite*, an animal the size of a pony, has a ropelike beak that it ropes the swiftest rabbits with.

The *Teakettler* gets its name from the noise it makes, resembling that of a boiling teakettle. Clouds of vapor issue from its mouth, it walks backward (from choice), and few woodsmen have ever seen one.

The head of the *Axehandle Hound* is shaped like an axe and its body looks like an axehandle. It has stubby little legs and all it will eat is axehandles.

Among the fish of the region is the *Upland Trout*, which builds its nests in trees, flies pretty well, and is afraid of water.

Then there is the *Goofang*, which swims backward so water won't get in its eyes. It's exactly the same size as the sunfish, only larger.

Nor should we forget the *Goofus Bird*, which builds its nest upside-down and flies backward, because it doesn't give a darn where it's going, it only wants to know where it's been.

The *Gillygaloo* used to build its nest on the slopes of the famous Pyramid Forty. It laid square eggs so they wouldn't roll down and break. Lumberjacks would hard-boil the eggs and use them for dice.

The *Pinnacle Grouse* had just one wing, so it could only fly in one direction, and it flew around one particular mountain day and night. The color of its plumage would change with the season and the condition of the observer.

The Chinese Fox

For the purposes of everyday zoology, the Chinese Fox is not greatly different from any other; for fantastic zoology, it is a very different creature. Statistics reveal that its lifespan varies from eight hundred to a thousand years. It is considered an animal of ill omen, and every part of its body is thought to possess a special virtue. It can cause fires by simply beating its tail against the ground, it is able to foresee the future, and it can take on many forms—it prefers that of an old man, a young damsel, or a scholar. It is cunning, wary, and skeptical; it gets great pleasure from doing mischief and during storms. When men die, they often transmigrate into the body of a Fox. Foxes live near graves. There are thousands of legends about the Fox; here is one that is not without its humor:

One day, Wang saw two Foxes standing on their hind legs, leaning against a tree. One of them was holding a piece of paper, and they were laughing as though sharing a joke. Wang tried to scare the Foxes away, but they stood firm; he then shot at the Fox holding the piece of paper. He wounded him in the eye and took the paper. In the inn, Wang told his adventure to the other guests. While he was talking, another gentleman came in, with a bad eye. He listened with interest to Wang's story, and then asked to see the paper. Wang was just about to show it to him when the innkeeper saw that the newcomer had a tail. "He's a Fox!" the innkeeper cried, and instantly the gentleman turned into a Fox, which ran out the door and fled. The Foxes tried repeatedly to recover the paper, which was covered with indecipherable characters, but they always failed. Wang decided to return home. On the road, he met his entire family, on their way to the capital. They told him that he himself had ordered them to undertake this journey, and his mother showed him the letter in which he asked them to sell all their property and meet him in the capital. Wang examined the letter and saw that it was a blank piece of paper. Though they now had not even a roof to cover their heads, Wang was adamant: "Let us return."

One day a younger brother of Wang's appeared, whom everyone thought was dead. He asked them how the family had fallen so low, and Wang told him the entire story. "Ah," said the brother, when Wang came to his adventure with the Foxes, "there is the root of all the evil." Wang showed him the document. Snatching it from his hand, the brother quickly stuffed it in his pocket. "At last I have recovered what I sought," he exclaimed, and turning into a Fox, ran away.

The Garuda

Vishnu, the second god of the trinity that rules over the Hindu pantheon, is often portrayed as riding on a serpent that fills the sea, but also sometimes on the bird named Garuda. Vishnu is portrayed as a blue deity, his four arms bearing a club, a seashell, a disc, and a lotus; Garuda is shown with the wings, head, and claws of an eagle and the torso and legs of a man. Its face is white, its wings crimson, and its body gold. Images of Garuda cast in bronze or sculpted in stone often crown the temple monoliths. In Gwalior there is one such statue that was erected by the Greek Heliodorus, a worshiper of Vishnu, more than a century before the Christian era.

In the *Garuda-Purana* (the seventeenth of the *Puranas*, the popular encyclopedia of ancient and medieval traditions of the Hindu religion), the learned bird instructs men in the origin of the universe, Vishnu's embodiment as the sun, the ceremonies associated with his worship, the eminent genealogies of the houses that trace their descent from the moon and sun, and the plot of the *Ramayana*, and it gives men diverse lessons in versification, grammar, and medicine.

In *Nagananda* (*The Joy of the Serpents*), a play composed by a seventh-century king, each day Garuda kills and devours a serpent, until one day a Buddhist prince teaches it the virtues of abstention. In the last act, the repentant creature brings back to life the bones of the serpents it has eaten. Eggeling suspects that this work is a Brahman satire on Buddhism.

Nimbarka, a mystic of uncertain date, has written that Garuda is a soul saved for all eternity; the crown, rings, and flute of the god are also souls.

Gnomes

nomes are more ancient than their name, which, though Greek, never appears in the classics, since it dates only from the sixteenth century. Etymologists attribute it to the Swiss alchemist Paracelsus, in whose writings it appears for the first time.

These creatures are elves of the earth and mountains. Folklore portrays them as bearded dwarves of harsh and grotesque features. They wear brown tights and monastic cowls. Like the Gryphons of Hellenic and Oriental superstition and the Dragons of Saxon lore, they are said to guard hidden treasures.

"Gnosis," in Greek, means "knowledge"; it has been conjectured that Paracelsus invented the word "gnome" because these creatures knew, and could reveal to men, the exact location of hidden metals.

The Golem

There can be nothing accidental in a book dictated by a divine intelligence, not even the number of its words or the order of their letters; this was the belief of the kabbalists, who in their zeal to penetrate God's arcana devoted themselves to counting, combining, and permuting the letters of Holy Writ. In the thirteenth century, Dante declared that every passage of the Bible had a fourfold meaning: the literal, the allegorical, the moral, and the anagogical. John Scotus Erigena had already affirmed that the meanings of the Scripture, more consistent with the idea of divinity, were infinite, like the colors of the peacock's tail.

The kabbalists would have approved of that verdict: one of the secrets they sought within the divine text was how to create living beings. It was said of demons that they could shape large, solid creatures like the camel, but not finely wrought, delicate ones, and Rabbi Eliezer denied them the ability to produce anything smaller than a grain of barley. "Golem" was the name given the man created out of a combination of letters; the word literally means "an amorphous or lifeless substance."

In the Talmud (Sanhedrin, 65b), we read:

> If the righteous desired it, they could be creators, for it is written that . . . [by means of the *Sefer Yetsirah*, Book of Creation*], Rabbah created a man, and sent him to Rab Zera. Rab Zera spoke to him, but received no answer. Therefore he said unto him: "Thou art a creature of the magicians. Return to thy dust."

*By means of mystic combinations of the Divine Name [Talmudic note].

R. Hanina and R. Oshaia spent every Sabbath eve in studying the "Laws of Creation," by means of which they created a third-grown calf,* and ate it.[†]

We owe the fame of the Golem in the West to the Austrian novelist Gustav Meyrink, who wrote the following words in the fifth chapter of his dreamlike work *Der Golem*:

> The original story harks back, so they say, to the seventeenth century. With the help of an ancient formula, a rabbi is said to have put together an automatic man and used it to help ring the bells in the Synagogue and for all kinds of other menial work. But he hadn't made it into a proper man; it was more like a kind of animated vegetable, really. What life it had, too, so the story runs, only derived from a magic prescription placed behind his teeth each day, that drew down to itself what was known as "the free sidereal strength of the universe." And as, one evening, before evening prayers, the rabbi forgot to take the prescription out of the Golem's mouth, the figure fell into a frenzy, and went raging through the streets like a roaring lion, seeking whom it might devour. At last the rabbi was able to secure it, and he then destroyed the formula. The figure fell to pieces. The only record

---

**I.e.*, a calf that has reached one-third of its full growth; others interpret: (i) in its third year; (ii) third born, fat [Talmudic note].

†Similarly, Schopenhauer writes: "On page 325 of the first volume of his *Zauberbibliothek* Horst summarizes in the following way the doctrine of the English visionary Jane Leade: 'Whosoever possesses magical power may, at his will, rule and renew the mineral, plant, and animal kingdoms; thus, if a few wizards came to an agreement, all Creation might return to its paradisal state.'" (*On the Will in Nature*, VII)

left of it was the miniature clay figure that was shown to the people within the old Synagogue.

Eleazar of Worms has preserved the formula for making a Golem. The details of the enterprise require twenty-three columns in folio and demand that the maker know "the alphabets of the two hundred twenty-one gates" that must be repeated over each of the Golem's organs. On its forehead one must tattoo the word "EMET" which means "truth." In order to destroy the creature, one would efface the first letter, leaving the word "MET," which means "death."

The Gryphon

"Winged monsters," Herodotus calls the Gryphons when he relates their constant war with the Arimaspi; Pliny is almost as imprecise when he speaks of the long ears and curved beak of these "fabulous birds" (X, 70). Perhaps the most detailed description of the Gryphon is given by the problematic Sir John Mandeville in Chapter 85 of his famous *Travels*:

> From this land [Turkey] go men to the land of Bacharia, where be full evil folk and full cruel. In that land be trees that bear wool, as though it were of sheep, whereof men make clothes and all things that may be made of wool.
>
> In that country be many hippotaynes that dwell sometimes in the water and sometime on the land. And they be half man and half horse, as I have said before. And they eat men when they may take them. . . .
>
> In that country be many griffins, more plenty than in any other country. Some men say that they have the body upward as an eagle and beneath as a lion; and truly they say sooth, that they be of that shape. But one griffin hath the body more great and is more strong than eight lions, of such lions as be on this half, and more great and stronger than an hundred eagles such as we have amongst us. For one griffin there will bear, flying to his nest, a great horse, if he may find him at the point, or two oxen yoked together as they go at the plough. For he hath his talons so

long and so large and great upon his feet, as though they were horns of great oxen or of bugles or of kine, so that men make cups of them to drink of. And of their ribs and of the pens of their wings, men make bows, full strong, to shoot with arrows and quarrels.

In Madagascar, another famous traveler, Marco Polo, heard tales of the *rukh*, or Roc, and at first understood them to refer to the *uccello grifone*, the Gryphon-bird (*Travels*, III, 36).

In the Middle Ages, the symbology of the Gryphon is contradictory. One Italian bestiary says that it stands for the devil; generally, however, it is the emblem of Christ, and thus it is explained by Isidore of Seville in his *Etymologies:* "Christ is Lion because he reigns and has strength; Eagle, because after the Resurrection He rises into Heaven."

In the twenty-ninth canto of the *Purgatorio*, Dante dreams of a

> Triumph-car, on two wheels travelling,
> And at the shoulders of a Gryphon drawn;
>
> . . .
>
> Golden of limb so far as he was bird,
> The rest all dappled red-and-white was he.

Commentators tell us that the leonine "dappled red-and-white" (to signify the flesh) combined with avian gold signifies the human nature of Christ.* Others understand Dante to have been symbolizing the Pope, who is priest and king. Didron, in his

---

*This recalls the description of the Spouse in the Song of Songs (5:10–11): "My beloved is white and ruddy. . . . His head is as the most fine gold."

Christian Iconography, writes that the "Pope, as pontiff or Eagle, is raised up to the throne of God to receive His commandments, and as Lion or king walks upon the Earth with strength and vigor."

The Hairy Beast of La Ferté-Bernard[*]

During the Middle Ages an animal known as La Velue, "the Hairy One," roamed the banks of the Huisne, an apparently tranquil stream, pillaging and marauding. This beast must have survived the Flood without having been taken into the Ark. It was the size of a bull, though it had the head of a serpent and a round body covered with shaggy green hair and bristling spines whose prick meant death to men. Its feet were broad, like a tortoise's; with its serpentine tail it would lash out at men and animals and kill them. When it grew angry, it would spew out crop-destroying fire. At night, it would invade the stables, and if the peasants pursued it, it would leap into the water of the Huisne to escape them, making the river's banks overflow and flood the countryside around.

Its preferred victims were innocents—maidens and children. It would choose the most virtuous maiden of the region, who would be called L'Agnelle, "the Lamb." One day, it snatched up a Little Lamb and dragged her off, torn and bloody, to the stream. The victim's betrothed followed La Velue to the Huisne and with his sword cut off the monster's tail, the only vulnerable part of its body. The beast died on the instant. The peasants embalmed the monster's body and celebrated its death with drums, fifes, and dancing.

[*]A French City on the Huisne.

Haniel, Kafziel, Azriel, and Aniel

In Babylon, Ezekiel had a vision of four "living creatures" or angels, "and every one had four faces, and every one had four wings," and "as for the likeness of their faces, they four had the face of a man, and the face of a lion, on the right side, and they four had the face of an ox on the left side: they four also had the face of an eagle." Ezekiel further tells us that "whither the spirit was to go, they went," and "when they went, they went upon their four sides" or faces, growing magically, perhaps, out into the four directions. Four wheels, "so high that they were dreadful," and "full of eyes round about them four," followed the angels.

Memories of Ezekiel inspired the animals of St. John's apocalyptic Revelations, in whose fourth chapter we read the following:

6 And before the throne there was a sea of glass like unto crystal: and in the midst of the throne, and round about the throne, were four beasts full of eyes before and behind.

7 And the first beast was like a lion, and the second beast like a calf, and the third beast had a face as a man, and the fourth beast was like a flying eagle.

8 And the four beasts had each of them six wings about him; and they were full of eyes within: and they rest not day and night, saying, Holy, holy, holy, Lord God Almighty, which was, and is, and is to come.

The *Zohar* (Book of Splendor) adds that the four animals are called Haniel, Kafziel, Azriel, and Aniel, and that they look to the east, the north, the south, and the west.

Stevenson wondered: If there were such things in Heaven, what, then, might there be in Hell? It is from that same passage in Revelations that Chesterton derived his famous metaphor for night: "a monster made of eyes."

The fourfold angels of the Book of Ezekiel are called "hayoth," or "living beings"; in the *Sefer Yetsirah*, they are the ten numbers that were used, like the twenty-two letters of the alphabet, to create this world; in the *Zohar* they are said to have descended from the higher spheres, crowned with letters.

From the four faces of the hayoth the symbols for the four evangelists were derived: Matthew was accorded the angel, sometimes human and bearded; Mark, the lion; Luke, the ox; John, the eagle. In his commentary on Ezekiel, St. Jerome attempted to apply reason to these attributions. He says that Matthew was given the figure of the angel (the man) because Matthew had emphasized Christ's humanity; Mark was assigned the lion because Mark declared Christ's royal dignity; Luke was assigned the ox, the emblem of sacrifice, because Luke stressed Christ's sacerdotal nature; and John, the eagle because he had insisted upon Christ's fervent ascent.

A German scholar, Dr. Richard Hennig, sees the remote origins of these signs in four signs of the zodiac at ninety-degree intervals. The lion and bull offer not the slightest difficulty; the angel has been associated with Aquarius, which has the face of a man; the eagle of John is then tied to Scorpio, though Scorpio is rejected because of its ominous connotations. In his *Dictionary of Astrology*, Nicholas DeVore puts forth this same hypothesis, observing that the four figures are joined in the figure of the Sphinx, which may have a human head, the body of a bull, the claws and tail of a lion, and the wings of an eagle.

Haokah, God of Thunder

Among the Sioux, Haokah used the winds as drumsticks with which to pound the Thunder Drum. His horns showed that he was also the god of the hunt. He wept when he was happy, and laughed when he was sad. He experienced cold as heat and heat as cold.

The Hare in the Moon

In the dark regions of the moon, the English see the face of a man; two or three references to the "Man in the Moon" may be found in Shakespeare's *Midsummer Night's Dream*. Shakespeare mentions the bundle of thorns carried by the man in the moon; some of the last lines of Canto XX of the *Inferno* speak of "Cain with his thorn-bush [striding] the sill / Of the two hemispheres." Tommaso Casini's commentary on these lines recalls a Tuscan fable: the Lord imprisoned Cain in the moon, where he was condemned to carry a bundle of thorns until the end of time.

Others see in the moon the Holy Family, and it was with that image in mind that Lugones, in his *Lunario sentimental*, wrote the following lines:

> *Y está todo: la Virgen con el niño; al flanco,*
> *San José (algunos tienen la buena fortuna*
> *De ver su vara); y el buen burrito blanco*
> *Trota que trota los campos de la luna.*

We might translate these lines this way:

> And there is all: the Virgin with the Child; beside,
> walks Joseph (some are giv'n the good fortune
> to see his staff); then the gentle burro, white,
> that trots through the landscape of the moon.

The Chinese, on the other hand, see in the moon a Hare. "Buddha," we are told, "in one of his former lives, was fed with the flesh of a Hare which leapt into a fire for that purpose, and he rewarded the animal by sending it to the moon." There, under an acacia tree, in a magic mortar, the Hare pounds the drugs that go into the elixir of life. In the popular speech of certain regions, this Hare is called "the doctor" or "precious" or "jadelike."

People believe that the common hare lives for a thousand years and turns white as it grows older.

The Harpies

In the *Theogony*, Hesiod tells us that the Harpies are winged deities "of lovely hair, who in the speed of their wings keep pace with the blowing winds, or birds in flight." In the third book of *The Æneid*, these creatures are portrayed as birds with the faces of women pale with a hunger they cannot sate, and with curved claws, and filthy bellies. They swoop down from the mountains and defile the food upon tables set for feasts. They are invulnerable, and fetid; they are all-devouring, shrieking creatures, and they turn everything in their path to excrement. Servius, one of Virgil's commentators, wrote that just as Hecate is Proserpine in Hades, Diana upon the earth, and Luna in Heaven, for which reason she is called the "triple goddess," so the Harpies are the Furies of the underworld, the Harpies of the earth, and the Diræ, or demons, of the sky. They are sometimes confused with the Fates.

By divine decree, the Harpies once beset a king of Thrace who had revealed the future to men or, perhaps, had traded his eyesight for long life and was punished by the sun, whose works the king had thereby insulted. As this king was making preparations for a banquet for his court, the Harpies flew down and devoured and defiled the delicacies that had been set out. The Argonauts managed to chase them away; Appolonius of Rhodes and William Morris (in *The Life and Death of Jason*) have retold the fantastic story. In Canto XXXIII of the *Furioso*, Ariosto turns the king of Thrace into Prester John, the fabulous emperor of the Abyssinians.

In Greek, the word "harpy" means "she who abducts," "she who swoops down and snatches away"—a raptor. At first, they were goddesses of the storm wind, like the Maruts of the Vedas, who wield weapons of gold (lightning bolts) and milk the clouds.

The Hippogriff

As a way of denoting impossibility or incongruence, Virgil spoke of "mating horses with Gryphons." Four hundred years later, Servius (one of Virgil's commentators) declared Gryphons to be eagles from the midpoint of their bodies upward and lions from the midpoint down. To make that statement even stronger, Servius added that these animals hate horses. . . . In time, the locution *iungentur iam grypes equis,* or "cross Gryphons with horses," became a common saying; in the early sixteenth century, Ludovico Ariosto recalled the phrase, and invented the Hippogriff. Eagle and lion commingle in the Gryphon of the ancients; in the Ariostan Hippogriff it is horse and Gryphon—a second-degree monster, or second-degree feat of imagination. Pietro Micheli points out, however, that it is a more "harmonious" beast than a winged horse.

A precise description of the Hippogriff, as though written on purpose for a dictionary of fantastic zoology, may be found in *Orlando Furioso.* The first mention of the strange beast is deceptively blasé: "When, as we journey by Rhone's current, I / A rider on a winged courser spy." Other octaves express more astonishment and wonder at the flying horse. This one is quite famous:

> *E vede l'oste e tutta la famiglia,*
> *E chi a finestre e chi fuor ne la via,*
> *Tener levati al ciel gli occhi e le ciglia,*
> *Come L'Ecclisse or la Cometa sia.*
> *Vede la Donna un'alta maraviglia,*
> *Che di leggier creduta non saria:*

Vede passar un gran destriero alato,
Che porta in aria un cavalliero armato.

W. S. Rose translates this stanza in the following way:

[Bradamant] sees the host and all his family,
Where, one to door, and one to window slips,
With eyes upturned and gazing at the sky,
As if to witness comet or eclipse.
And there the lady views, with wondering eye,
What she had scarce believed from other's lips—
A feathered courser, sailing through the rack,
Who bore an armed knight upon his back.

In one of the final cantos, Astolpho takes the saddle off the Hippogriff and sets it free.

Hochigan

Descartes tells us that monkeys could talk if they wanted to, but they have decided to keep silent so that humans will not force them to work. The Bushmen of South Africa believe that there was a time when all animals could talk. Hochigan hated animals; one day it disappeared, taking the gift of speech with it.

Humbaba

Well might we ask what shape was taken by the gigantic Humbaba (or Khumbaba or Huwawa) that guarded the Mountain of Cedars in the Babylonian epic *Gilgamesh*. In his German translation of the fragmentary epic, perhaps the oldest epic in the world, George Burckhardt attempted to reconstruct the monster; this is his description, translated into English:

Enkidu with an axe felled one of the cedars. "Who has come into the Forest and felled a cedar tree?" an enormous voice asked. The heroes saw Khumbaba advance upon them. It had the claws of a lion; its body was covered with rough brassy scales. Its feet were the talons of a vulture, and on its forehead it wore the horns of a savage bull. The tail and generative organ of the monster ended in the head of a serpent.

In the ninth canto of *Gilgamesh,* scorpion beings, half scorpion, half human—creatures whose heads brush up against the Heavens, while their udders hang down into the shadows of the Cavern of the Earth—guard the door in the mountains through which the sun emerges each morning.

The poem is in twelve parts, which correspond to the twelve signs of the zodiac.

The Hundred-Heads

The Hundred-Heads is a fish created out of a few words' karma by posthumous repercussions down through time. One of the Chinese biographies of the Buddha says that one day the Buddha encountered some fishermen pulling in their nets. After endless effort, they dragged up on shore an enormous fish, with one head a monkey's, another a dog's, another a horse's, another a fox's, another a pig's, another a tiger's, and so on, to the number of one hundred.

"Are you not Kapila?" the Buddha asked the fish.

"I am Kapila," the Hundred-Heads answered, and then died.

The Buddha explained to his disciples that in a previous incarnation, Kapila had been a Brahmin who had become a monk, and surpassed all men in his knowledge of the sacred texts. Sometimes his companions would make mistakes, at which Kapila would call them "monkey-head," "dog-head," etc. When he died, the karma of that accumulated invective made him come back to life as a sea monster, floundering under the weight of all the heads he had wished upon his companions.

The Hydra

Typhon (the hideous son of Earth and Tartarus) fathered upon Echidna, "half . . . lovely woman, half . . . speckled serpent," the creature we call the Hydra, "a many-headed water-serpent living at Lerna." The historian Diodorus gives the Hydra a hundred heads; Appolodorus' *Encyclopedia* gives it nine. Lemprière tells us that nine is in fact the most commonly accepted number. The horrible thing about the creature, whatever number we may credit, is that when one head is cut off, two spring up in its place. Some have said that the heads were human, and that the one in the center was eternal. The creature's breath poisoned the waters and brought drought to the fields. Even when it slept, the venom in the air around it could mean death to a man. "Hera [Juno] reared it," we are told by Graves, "as a menace to Herakles."

This serpent seemed fated to live forever. Its den was among the swamps of Lerna, to which Hercules was driven in his chariot by Iolaus to seek it out. There, as Hercules cut off its heads, Iolaus seared the wounds with a torch, checking the flow of blood. Hercules buried the last head, which was immortal, under a huge rock, and there where he buried it, it still lies today, hating and dreaming.

In other adventures with other beasts, wounds from the arrows that Hercules had dipped in the Hydra's gall invariably proved fatal.

A crab, the ally of the Hydra, nipped at Hercules' foot, but Hercules furiously crushed it with his heel. Juno raised the crab into the sky and set it among the stars; today it is the constellation and sign of Cancer.

Ichthyocentaurs

L icofronte, Claudianus, and the Byzantine grammarian John Tzetzes have each, separately, mentioned the Ichthyocentaurs; there is no other reference to them in the classics. We might translate their name as "Centaur-Fish"; the word was applied to beings that mythologers have also termed Centaur-Tritons. They are often portrayed in Roman and Hellenistic sculpture. From the waist up, they are men; from the waist down, they are fish, and their forefeet are those of horse or lion. They have their place among the sea gods, alongside the Hippocampuses.

The Jinn

Islamic tradition holds that Allah created angels from light, Jinn (singular "jinnee") from fire, and men from dust. Some contend that the Jinn were formed out of a dark and smokeless fire. They were created two thousand years before Adam, but their race, Lane tells us, shall "die before the general resurrection."

Lane offers us the following further information on this race:

> "It is held," says El-Kazweenee, a writer of the thirteenth century, "that the Jinn are aërial animals, with transparent bodies, which can assume various forms."

They make themselves visible at first as clouds or tall undefined pillars; then, according to their desire, they take the form of men, jackals, wolves, lions, scorpions, or serpents. Some are believers; others, infidels—heretics or atheists. Before a person kills a serpent, one should admonish it, in the name of the Prophet, to depart the chamber it has entered; it may be killed if it does not obey. Jinn are able to pass through thick walls or fly through the air or suddenly become invisible. "They often ascend to the confines of the lowest heaven," Lane tells us, "and there, listening to the conversation of the Angels respecting things decreed by God, obtain knowledge of futurity, which they sometimes impart to men, who, by means of talismans, or certain invocations, make them to serve the purposes of magical performances." Some scholars say that the Jinn (or one of them) built the pyramids of Egypt, and also, by order of Suleyman (Solomon), who knew the Most Great Name of God, the Temple of Jerusalem.

Jinn are said to station themselves on the roofs or at the windows of houses and throw down bricks and stones on persons passing by; they also carry off beautiful women to be their wives or concubines. To keep them off and secure one's property against such depredations, one is counseled to repeat the words "In the name of God, the Compassionate, the Merciful!" Their most common dwelling places are ruins, uninhabited houses, wells, rivers, and deserts. The Egyptians say that the Jinn are the cause of whirlwinds of sand or dust that rise like pillars in the desert; they also believe that shooting stars are spears hurled by Allah at evil Jinn.

Iblis is their sire and leader.

The Kami

According to Seneca, Thales of Miletus taught that the earth floats upon the water like a ship, and that the water, agitated by storms, causes earthquakes. A different cause is proposed by the Japanese historians (or mythologers) of the eighth century. On one famous page, we read the following:

> Now beneath the Fertile-Land-of-Reed-Plains lay a Kami [a supernatural being] in the form of a great cat-fish, and by its movement it caused the earth to quake, till the Great Deity of Deer-Island thrust his sword deep into the earth and transfixed the Kami's head. So, now, when the evil Kami is violent, [the Emperor Young-Three-Hairs-Moor] puts forth his hand and lays it upon the sword till the Kami becomes quiet.

(The haft of the sword, carved from stone, sticks out of the earth a few steps from the temple of Kashima. One feudal lord dug for six days and six nights without reaching the tip of the blade.)

Post Wheeler, who transcribed the legend of the catfishlike Kami, also tells us of "the Jinshin-Uwo, or Earthquake Fish, [which] is popularly believed to have a body like that of an eel, . . . to be seven hundred miles long and to hold Japan on its back, its head being beneath K'yoto and its tail beneath Awomori, in the north. In some sections its head is believed to be beneath the northern part of the main island of the archipelago (where earthquakes seldomest occur) and its tail beneath the Province of Shinano." (Clearly a rationalist inversion, for it is easier to imagine a movement of the tail than of the head.) This animal is vaguely analogous to the legendary Arabian Bahamut and the Mithgarthsworm (or Earth Serpent) of the Eddas, for when the Mithgarthsworm "wallows in giant-rage," the sea rushes up on the land and "shaggy hills shiver."

"In some sections," Wheeler continues, "local legend substitutes [without appreciable advantage, we might say] the Earthquake Beetle (*Jinshin-Mushi*) with a dragon's head, ten spider-legs, and a scaly body, which lives deep in the earth" rather than under the sea.

A King of Fire and His Steed

Heraclitus taught that the first element was fire, but that is not the same as imagining *beings* of fire, beings carved from the momentary and changing stuff of flame. This almost impossible image was, however, attempted by William Morris in his tale "The Ring Given to Venus" in the poem-cycle *The Earthly Paradise* (1868–1870). These are the lines in question:

> Most like a mighty king was he,
> And crowned and sceptered royally;
> As a white flame his visage shone,
> Sharp, clear-cut as a face of stone;
> But flickering flame, not flesh, it was;
> And over it such looks did pass
> Of wild desire, and pain, and fear,
> As in his people's faces were,
> But tenfold fiercer: furthermore,
> A wondrous steed the Master bore,
> Unnameable of kind or make,
> Not horse, nor hippogriff, nor drake,
> Like and unlike to all of these,
> And flickering like the semblances
> Of an ill dream . . . °

In these lines we may perhaps detect the influence of that deliberately ambiguous personification of death in *Paradise Lost* (II, 666–73):

The other shape,
If shape it might be call'd, that shape had none
Distinguishable in member, joint, or limb,
Or substance might be call'd that shadow seem'd,
For each seem'd either; black it stood as night,
Fierce as ten furies, terrible as hell,
And shook a dreadful dart; what seem'd his head
The likeness of a kingly crown had on.

The Kraken

The Kraken is a Scandinavian species of the Zarathan and the Arabian Sea Dragon or Sea Snake.

In 1752, the Danish bishop of Bergen, Erich Pontoppidan, published his *Natural History of Norway*, a work famed for its hospitality (or credulity); among its pages, one may read that the Kraken has a hump a mile and a half long, and arms that can encircle the largest ship. The hump rises out of the sea like an island; Erich Pontoppidan goes so far as to formulate this rule: "Floating islands are always Krakens." He also writes that the Kraken often turns the waters of the ocean murky with a liquid it discharges; this statement has caused some to surmise that the Kraken is a magnification of the octopus or squid.

Among Tennyson's juvenilia, there is a poem dedicated to the Kraken. It reads as follows:

THE KRAKEN
Below the thunders of the upper deep;
Far, far beneath in the abysmal sea,
His ancient, dreamless, uninvaded sleep
The Kraken sleepeth: faintest sunlights flee
About his shadowy sides: above him swell
Huge sponges of millennial growth and height;
And far away into the sickly light,
From many a wondrous grot and secret cell
Unnumber'd and enormous polypi
Winnow with giant arms the slumbering green.
There hath he lain for ages and will lie

Battening upon huge seaworms in his sleep,
Until the latter fire shall heat the deep;
Then once by man and angels to be seen,
In roaring he shall rise and on the surface die.

Kronos or Herakles

In his treatise *Difficulties and Solutions of First Principles*, the
Neoplatonist Damascius of Syria records a curious variant of
Orphic theogony and cosmogony in which Kronos (or Her-
akles) is a monster:

> According to Hieronymus and Hellanicus (if indeed the
> two authors were not one), Orphic doctrine teaches that in
> the beginning there was water and also that matter out of
> which the earth was formed. There were, then, at first two
> principles: water and earth. . . . After them, and from them,
> emerged a third principle, a dragon, having the heads of a
> bull and a lion joined together—in the center of its body,
> the visage of a god, provided with wings upon its shoulders.
> This creature was called "Kronos, who does not grow old,"
> and also "Herakles." To accompany this creature, *Anaké*
> [Necessity, called also The Inevitable] was born, having an
> incorporeal nature that spreads throughout the Universe
> and touches its two borders. . . . According to this theol-
> ogy, certainly, Kronos is the Dragon, and from him are
> born three things, called by this theology intellectual
> Ether, infinite Chaos, and cloudlike Erebus. Under these,
> Kronos set the seed of an egg, from which the world
> would emerge. This last principle was an incorporeal god
> which was both male and female, with wings of gold upon
> its back and the head of a bull upon each thigh, and upon
> its head an immense dragon, like all manner of wild
> beasts.

Perhaps because the huge and monstrous seems less appropriate to Greece than to the Orient, Walter Kranz attributes Eastern origins to these images.

The Lamed Wufniks

On the earth there are, and have always been, thirty-six just men whose mission is to justify the world to God. These are the Lamed Wufniks. These men do not know each other, and they are very poor. If a man comes to realize that he is a Lamed Wufnik, he immediately dies and another man, perhaps in some other corner of the earth, takes his place. These men are, without suspecting it, the secret pillars of the universe. If not for them, God would annihilate the human race. They are our saviors, though they do not know it.

This mystical belief of the Jewish people has been explained by Max Brod.

Its distant roots may be found in Genesis 18, where God says that He will not destroy the city of Sodom if ten just men can be found within it.

The Arabs have an analogous figure, the Qutb, or "saint."

The Lamia

According to the Latin and Greek classics, the Lamia lived in Africa. From the waist up, their bodies took the form of a beautiful woman; below, that of a serpent. Some reports have called them sorceresses; others, malign monsters. They lacked the faculty of speech, but their whistling was melodious. They would lure travelers to themselves in the desert, and then devour them. Their remote origins were divine; they sprang from one of Zeus's many amours. In that part of the *Anatomy of Melancholy* (1621) that treats of the passion of love, Robert Burton tells the story of a Lamia that assumed human form and seduced a young philosopher, "taking him home to her house in the suburbs of Corinth":

> She being fair and lovely would live and die with him, that was fair and lovely to behold. The young man tarried with her a while to his great content, and at last married her, to whose wedding came Apollonius, who by some probable conjectures found her out to be a Serpent, a Lamia. When she saw herself descried, she wept, and desired Apollonius to be silent, but he would not be moved, and thereupon plate, house, and all that was in it, vanished in an instant.

Shortly before his death, John Keats (1795–1821) was inspired by Burton's tale to write his poem "Lamia."

The Lemuri

These creatures were also called larvæ. Unlike the household Lares, which protected the members of the family, the Lemuri were souls of the evil dead that wandered the world inspiring terror in men. They tortured the impious and the just alike. The Rome of the pre-Christian era held celebrations in their honor in the month of May; these feasts were called lamurias, and were instituted by Romulus in order to pacify the soul of Remus, whom he had executed. An epidemic had devastated Rome, and the oracle consulted by Romulus had counseled him to hold these annual feasts, which lasted for three nights. The temples of other deities were closed during this time, and weddings were forbidden. It was customary to scatter beans on graves, or cast them into the fire, since smoke warded off the Lemuri. They were also frightened away by drums and magical words. The curious reader may find further report of these creatures in the pages of Ovid's *Fasti.*

The Leveler

etween 1840 and 1864, the Father of Light (who is also called the Inner Word) afforded the musician and pedagogue Jakob Lorber a series of protracted revelations concerning the humanity, the fauna, and the flora of the celestial bodies that make up our solar system. One of the domestic animals that those revelations apprised us of is the Leveler, or Tamper-Downer (*Bodendrucker*), which renders incalculable services on the planet Miron (identified by the current editor of Lorber's work as Neptune).

The Leveler is ten times larger than the elephant, which it greatly resembles. It has a shortish trunk, long straight tusks,

and pale green skin. Its legs are very thick, and they are conical; the points of the cones seem to fit into its body. The Leveler is a plantigrade animal that labors for bricklayers and builders to level the ground: it is led to a plot of uneven ground, and with its legs, its trunk, and its tusks, it levels it.

The Leveler feeds upon grass and roots and has no enemies, save a few species of insects.

The Offspring of Leviathan

At that time, on the shores of the Rhone River, in a forest which lay between Arles and Avignon, there dwelt a Dragon, which was half animal and half fish, larger than an ox, longer than a horse, with teeth like swords and as sharp as horns, and two bucklers on each side of his body: and this beast lurked in the river, and slew the passersby, and sank the ships. He had come by sea from Galatia in Asia, and was engendered of the Leviathan, which is a most ferocious serpent living in the ocean, and of the Onager, an animal which dwells in the region of Galatia, and which shoots its ordure like a bolt at all who are within the space of an acre, and everything which is touched thereby is consumed as with fire.

—*La légende dorée*, Lyon, 1518.

Lilith

"For before Eve there was Lilith," reads a Hebrew text. This creature's legend inspired the English poet Dante Gabriel Rossetti (1828–1882) to compose his "Eden Bower."

Lilith was a serpent; she was Adam's first wife and gave him "glittering sons and radiant daughters." Then, God created Eve; as revenge on Adam's human wife, Lilith persuaded her to taste the forbidden fruit and to bear Cain, Abel's brother and his murderer. That is the primitive form of the myth that was followed by Rossetti. Down through the Middle Ages, under the influence of the Hebrew word *layil*, which means "night," little by little the myth became transformed: Lilith was no longer a serpent; she became a spirit of the night. Sometimes she was an angel that ruled over the procreation of man; sometimes she was demons that attacked those who slept alone or walked alone at night. In the popular imagination she often assumes the form of a tall, silent woman with long black hair.

The Mandrake

L ike the Borametz, the plant called the Mandrake (or Mandragora) shares certain characteristics with the creatures of the animal kingdom, for it shrieks when it is pulled from the ground; that scream has the ability to drive those who hear it mad (*Romeo and Juliet*, IV:3). Pythagoras, Sir Thomas Browne tells us in his *Pseudodoxia Epidemica* (1646), calls the Mandrake "Anthropomorphus"; the Latin agronomist Lucius Columella "tearms it *semihomo*," and Albertus Magnus "affirmeth that Mandrakes represent mankinde, with the distinction of either sex." Before these writers, Pliny (who called the plant the Mandragora) had said that "the white Mandragora is . . . the male plant and the black, . . . the female"; he also said that those "about to gather this plant, after tracing three circles round it with a sword, turn towards the west and dig it up. . . . The very odour of [the leaves] is highly oppressive . . . and persons . . . are apt to be struck dumb by the odour of this plant." The last book of Flavius Josephus' *History of the Jewish War* counsels that a trained dog be used "if persons taking it up would avoid dreadful misfortunes."

The purportedly human form of the Mandrake suggested the superstition that it grows at the foot of gallows. Sir Thomas Browne speaks of the "fat or urine that drops from the body" of the hanged man; the popular novelist Hanns Heinz Ewers (*Alraune*, 1913) mentions the hanged man's semen. In German, Mandrake is "*Alraune*"; earlier, it was "*Alruna*." The word comes from "rune," which means "mystery," "occult thing," and later was applied to the characters of the first Germanic alphabet.

Genesis (30:14–16) includes a curious reference to the generative properties of the Mandrake. In the twelfth century, a Judeo-German commentator of the Talmud wrote this paragraph:

> A kind of cord emerges from a root upon the ground, and to the cord is joined by the navel, as though it were a melon, an animal called the Yadu'a, but the Yadu'a is in all ways like men: face, body, hands, and feet. It uproots and destroys all things all around, out to the limit of the cord. One must sunder the cord with an arrow, and then the animal dies.

Discorides identified the Mandrake with the Circea, or "Circean herb," of which we may read in the tenth book of *The Odyssey* the following:

> [Hermes] bent down glittering for the magic plant
> and pulled it up, black root and milky flower—
> fatigue and pain for mortals to uproot;
> but gods do this, and everything, with ease.

The Mantichora, or Manticore

Pliny (VIII, 30) tells us that "among these same Æthiopians, there is an animal found, which [Ctesias, the Greek physician to Artaxerxes Mnemon] calls the Mantichora; it has a triple row of teeth, which fit into each other like those of a comb, the face and ears of a man, and azure eyes, is of the colour of blood, has the body of the lion, and a tail ending in a sting, like that of the scorpion. Its voice resembles the union of the sound of the flute and the trumpet; it is of excessive swiftness, and is particularly fond of human flesh."

Flaubert has improved upon this description, as we read in the last pages of his *Temptation of St. Anthony*:

THE MARTICHORAS [*sic*]
(*A gigantic red lion, with human face, and three rows of teeth*):

"The gleam of my scarlet hair mingles with the reflection of the great sands. I breathe through my nostrils the terror of solitudes. I spit forth plague. I devour armies when they venture into the desert.

"My claws are twisted like screws, my teeth shaped like saws; and my curving tail bristles with darts which I cast to right and left, before and behind!

"See! see!"

(*The Martichoras shoots forth the keen bristles of his tail, which irradiate in all directions like a volley of arrows. Drops of blood rain down, spattering upon the foliage.*)

The Minotaur

The idea of a house built expressly so that people will become lost in it may be stranger than the idea of a man with the head of a bull, and yet the two ideas may reinforce one another. Indeed, the image of the Labyrinth and the image of the Minotaur seem to "go together": it is fitting that at the center of a monstrous house there should live a monstrous inhabitant.

The Minotaur, half man, half bull, was born out of the lovemaking of Pasiphaë, the queen of Crete, with a white bull sent by Poseidon from the sea. Dædalus, the artificer who built the device that allowed such a passion to be consummated, also built the Labyrinth destined to house, and hide, the monstrous offspring. The Minotaur ate human flesh; to satisfy its hunger, the king of Crete required that Athens render Crete a yearly tribute of seven youths and seven maidens. Theseus resolved to save his kingdom from that terrible taxation, and volunteered to go. Ariadne, the daughter of the king, gave the young man a spool of thread so that he would not become lost in the mazy corridors of the Labyrinth; the hero killed the Minotaur and followed the thread out of the maze.

Ovid, in an attempt at a witty turn of phrase, speaks of the "man half bull and the bull half man"; Dante, who was familiar with the words of the ancients but not with their coins and monuments, pictured the Minotaur with the head of a man and the body of a bull (*Inferno*, XII, 1–30).

The worship of the bull and the double-headed axe (whose name was *labrys*, and so might well have evolved into "labyrinth") was characteristic of pre-Hellenic religions, which held sacred festivals in their honor, known as Tauromachias. To judge from murals, human figures with the heads of bulls figured in Cretan demonology. The Greek fable of the Minotaur is probably a late and somewhat uncouth version of very ancient myths—the shadow of other, still more horrific, dreams.

The Ink Monkey

This animal is common in the northern regions and is about four or five inches long; it is endowed with an unusual instinct; its eyes are like carnelian stones, and its hair is jet black, sleek and flexible, as soft as a pillow. It is very fond of eating thick China ink, and whenever people write, it sits with folded hands and crossed legs, waiting till the writing is finished, when it drinks up the remainder of the ink; which done, it squats down as before; and does not frisk about unnecessarily.

—Wang Tai-hai (1791)

The Mother of Tortoises

Twenty-two hundred years before Christ, the fair-handed emperor known as the Great Yü wandered the Nine Mountains, Nine Rivers, and Nine Swamplands, measuring them with his paces; he divided the earth into nine regions suited for virtue and agriculture. Thus did he restrain the waters that threatened to flood the sky and the earth, and historians tell us that the divisions he imposed upon the world of men were revealed to him by a supernatural or angelic Tortoise that crawled up out of a riverbed. There are those who claim that this reptile, the Mother of all Tortoises, was made of fire and water; others claim for the creature a much less common substance—the light of the stars that make up the constellation Sagittarius. Upon the Tortoise's shell, it is said, there was written a cosmic treatise called the *Hong Fan* (General Rule) or a diagram of the Nine Subdivisions of that treatise, and it was written in black and white dots.

The Chinese believe that the sky is a hemisphere and that the earth has four corners; that is why they see the Tortoise as an image or model of the universe. Tortoises, moreover, are as long-lived as the cosmos; it is only natural that they should be included among the "spiritual" animals, along with the Unicorn, the Dragon, the Phoenix, and the Tiger, and that fortune-tellers should scrutinize their shells for auguries.

Than-Qui (Tortoise-Genius) is the name of the Tortoise that revealed the *Hong Fan* to the emperor.

The Myrmecoleon

The Myrmecoleon is an inconceivable animal defined in the following way by Gustave Flaubert, who calls it Myrmecoles: "lion before and ant behind, whose genitals are set reversely." The history of this monster is interesting. In the Scriptures (Job 4:11), we read that "the old lion perisheth for lack of prey." The word in the Hebrew text translated as "lion" is *layish;* this anomalous word would seem to require an equally anomalous translation; the Seventy remembered an Arabian lion that Elianus and Strabo had called *myrmex,* and they coined the word "myrmecoleon." After several hundred years, this derivation was lost. In Greek, *myrmex* means "ant"; from those enigmatic words "the old [ant-]lion perisheth from lack of prey" there emerged a fantasy which medieval bestiaries propagated yet further:

> The *Physiologus* said [of this creature]: "Its father has the form of a lion, and its mother that of an ant. Its father eats flesh, but its mother grains. If then they engender the ant-lion, they engender a thing of two natures, such that it cannot eat flesh because of the nature of its mother, nor grains because of the nature of its father. It perishes, therefore, because it has no nutriment."

The Nagas

The Nagas belong to the mythologies of Hindustan; they are serpents, but often assume human shape.

In one of the books of the *Mahabharata*, Ulupi, the son of a Naga king, forces his affections upon Arjuna, though she wishes to keep her vow of chastity. The maiden reminds Ulupi that it is his duty to aid the unfortunate, and the hero concedes her one night. Buddha, meditating beneath his fig tree, is lashed by the wind and rain; a Naga, taking pity upon him, winds about the Buddha seven times and spreads its seven heads above the Buddha like a canopy. The Buddha then converts the Naga to his religion.

In his *Histoire du bouddhisme dans l'Inde*, Kern defines the Nagas as serpents resembling clouds. They live under the earth, in deep palaces. Followers of the religion of the Great Vehicle say that the Buddha preached one law to men and another to the gods, and that this latter law—esoteric law—was locked away in the heavens and palaces of the serpents, who delivered it, hundreds of years later, to the monk Nagarjuna.

Here is a legend picked up in India by the pilgrim Fa Hsien in the early fifth century:

> The king Asoka came to a lake near which there was a tower. He decided to destroy the tower in order to build a taller one. A Brahman led him into the tower, and once inside he said to him:
>
> "My human form is an illusion; I am really a Naga, a dragon. Because of my evil *karma* I have received this Naga body; by religious service I desire to atone for and

efface my guilt. You may destroy this sanctuary if you think yourself able to build another better one."

He then showed the king the vessels of the sanctuary. The king looked at them in alarm, for they were unlike anything seen amongst men, and he changed his mind.

The Nisnas

Among the monsters described in Flaubert's *Temptation of St. Anthony* are the Nisnas, which "have only one eye, one cheek, one hand, one leg, half a body, half a heart." One commentator, Jean-Claude Margolin, claims that Flaubert invented these creatures, but in the first volume of Lane's translation of *The Thousand and One Nights* (1839), they are said to be "the offspring of a Shikk [a demon] and a human being." The Nesnás, as Lane spells its name, is "half a human being; having half a head, half a body, one arm, and one leg, with which it hops with much agility; [it is] found in Hadramot and in the woods of El-Yemen, and [is] endowed with speech." Someone came upon one of these creatures, Lane reports: "It had but half a face, which was in its breast* and a tail like that of a sheep. The people of Hadramot, it is added, eat it; and its flesh is sweet. . . . A kind of Nesnás is also described as inhabiting the Island of Ráïj,† in the Sea of Es-Seen (China), and having wings like those of the bat." Lane does, however, scruple to include the following words: "'God,' the incredulous informant adds, 'is all-knowing.'"

*Like the Blemmyae [Lane].
†Perhaps Borneo [Lane].

The Norns

In medieval Norse mythology, the Norns were the Fates. Snorri Sturluson, who brought order to that inchoate mythology in the early thirteenth century, tells us that there are three principal Norns, whose names are Past, Present, and Future. It seems likely that this assertion is a refinement (or addition) of a theological nature; the ancient Germanic tribes were not generally given to such abstractions. Snorri portrays three maidens beside a fountain at the foot of the great tree Yggdrasil, which is the world. They inexorably weave our fate.

Time (the stuff of which these creatures were made) gradually forgot these maidens, but in 1606 William Shakespeare wrote his tragedy *Macbeth*, in the first scene of which they reappear. They are the three Witches who foretell the fate that awaits the soldiers. Shakespeare calls them the "Weird Sisters," which is as much as to say "the Fates." Wyrd, for the Anglo-Saxon people, was the silent deity that presided over both mortals and immortals.

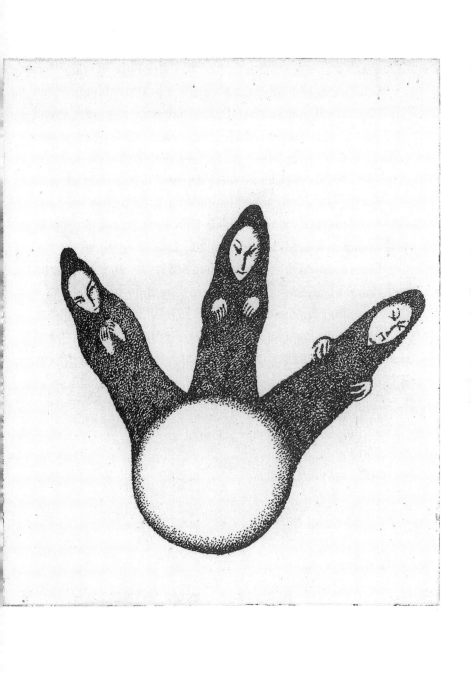

Nymphs

Paracelsus would have it that they live only in water, but the ancients divided the Nymphs into Water Nymphs and Land Nymphs. Some of these latter beings were Wood Nymphs, the presiding deities of woods and groves: the Hamadryads lived, invisible, inside trees, and died when the trees died. Other types of Nymphs were believed to be immortal, or to live for thousands of years. Those who lived in the sea were called Oceanids or Nereids; those who lived in rivers, Naiads. Their exact number is not known, but Hesiod ventured the figure three thousand. They were grave and lovely maidens; seeing them might bring on madness or, if they were naked, death; a line from Propertius avows that fact.

The ancients brought the Nymphs offerings of honey, oil, and milk. They were minor deities; no temples were built to them.

Odradek* by Kafka

Some say the word Odradek is of Slavonic origin, and try to account for it on that basis. Others again believe it to be of German origin, only influenced by Slavonic. The uncertainty of both interpretations allows one to assume with justice that neither is accurate, especially as neither of them provides an intelligent meaning of the word.

No one, of course, would occupy himself with such studies if there were not a creature called Odradek. At first glance it looks like a flat star-shaped spool for thread, and indeed it does seem to have thread wound upon it; to be sure, they are only old, broken-off bits of thread, knotted and tangled together, of the most varied sorts and colors. But it is not only a spool, for a small wooden crossbar sticks out of the middle of the star, and another small rod is joined to that at a right angle. By means of this latter rod on one side and one of the points of the star on the other, the whole thing can stand upright as if on two legs.

One is tempted to believe that the creature once had some sort of intelligible shape and is now only a broken-down remnant. Yet this does not seem to be the case; at least there is no sign of it; nowhere is there an unfinished or unbroken surface to suggest anything of the kind; the whole thing looks senseless enough, but in its own way perfectly finished. In any case, closer scrutiny is impossible, since Odradek is extraordinarily nimble and can never be laid hold of.

---

*Originally titled *"Die Sorge des Hausvaters"* ("The Cares of a Family Man").

He lurks by turns in the garret, the stairway, the lobbies, the entrance hall. Often for months on end he is not to be seen; then he has presumably moved into other houses; but he always comes faithfully back to our house again. Many a time when you go out of the door and he happens just to be leaning directly beneath you against the banisters you feel inclined to speak to him. Of course, you put no difficult questions to him, you treat him— he is so diminutive that you cannot help it—rather like a child. "Well, what's your name?" you ask him. "Odradek," he says. "And where do you live?" "No fixed abode," he says and laughs; but it is only the kind of laughter that has no lungs behind it. It sounds rather like the rustling of fallen leaves. And that is usually the end of the conversation. Even these answers are not always forthcoming; often he stays mute for a long time, as wooden as his appearance.

I ask myself, to no purpose, what is likely to happen to him? Can he possibly die? Anything that dies has had some kind of aim in life, some kind of activity, which has worn out; but that does not apply to Odradek. Am I to suppose, then, that he will always be rolling down the stairs, with ends of thread trailing after him, right before the feet of my children, and my children's children? He does no harm to anyone that one can see; but the idea that he is likely to survive me I find almost painful.

—Franz Kafka

One-Eyed Beings

In Spanish, the English word "monocle" is rendered "*monóculo.*" Before this word was used as the name of an eyeglass, it was applied to those men or creatures that had but a single eye. Thus, in a sonnet composed in the early seventeenth century, Góngora spoke of what we might translate as the "monocle'd suitor of Galatea." He was referring, of course, to Polyphemus, and in his *Fábula* he dedicated to that monster lines that exaggerate, but do not compare to, those (praised by Quintilian) in the third book of *The Æneid*—which in turn exaggerate but fall short of those lines in *The Odyssey*, Book IX. This literary decline corresponds to a decline in poetic faith: Virgil attempts to impress the reader with his Polyphemus though he hardly believes in him, while Góngora believes only in the Word—verbal artifice, verbal creatures.

The race of Cyclops was not the only one-eyed race; Pliny (VII, 2) mentions also the Arimaspi:

> [Not] far from the spot from which the north wind arises, the Arimaspi are said to exist, a nation remarkable for having but one eye, and that placed in the middle of the forehead. This race is said to carry on a perpetual warfare with the Griffins, a kind of monster, with wings, as they are commonly represented, for the gold which they dig out of the mines, and which these wild beasts retain and keep watch over with a singular degree of cupidity, while the Arimaspi are equally desirous to get possession of it.

Five hundred years earlier, the first encyclopedist, Herodotus of Halicarnassus, wrote the following (III, 116):

> Then again towards the North of Europe, there is evidently a quantity of gold by far larger than in any other land: as to how it is got, here again I am not able to say for certain, but it is said to be carried off from the griffins by Arimaspians, a one-eyed race of men. But I do not believe this tale either, that nature produces one-eyed men which in all other respects are like other men.

The Ouroboros

Today the ocean is a sea or system of seas; for the Greeks, Oceanus was a circular river that girdled the earth. All waters flowed from it, and it had neither outlet nor source. It was also a god or a Titan, perhaps the oldest of all, for Sleep, in Book XIV of *The Iliad*, calls Oceanus he "from whom all gods arose." In Hesiod's *Theogony*, Oceanus is the father of "the swirling rivers," which number three thousand, and foremost of which are Neilos (the Nile) and Alpheios. Oceanus was customarily portrayed as an old man with a full, flowing beard; after many centuries humanity discovered a better symbol.

Heraclitus had said that in the circle, the beginning and end are a single point. A third-century Greek amulet, to be found today in the British Museum, gives us an image that can better illustrate that infinitude: the serpent that bites its own tail or, as a Spanish poet put it, "that begins at the tip of its tail." Ouroboros ("he who devours his tail") is this monster's technical name, later employed in myriad texts by the alchemists.

This creature's most famous appearance is in Norse cosmogony. In the Younger, or Prose, Edda, Loki is said to have engendered a Wolf and a Serpent. An oracle warned the gods that these creatures would be the earth's doom. The Wolf, Fenrir, was bound by a "fetter called Gleipnir, made from six things: the noise a cat makes when it moves, the beard of woman, the roots of a mountain, the sinews of a bear, the breath of a fish, and the spittle of a bird." The Serpent, Jörmungandr, the "Mithgarth-Serpent," "was flung into the deep sea which surrounds the whole world, and it grew so large that it now lies in the middle of the ocean round the earth, biting its own tail."

In Jotunheim, or "Giant-Land," Utgarda-Loki once challenged the god Thor to lift a cat; Thor, using all his strength, could barely lift one of the cat's paws off the ground; this cat was Jörmun- gandr, and Thor was tricked by magic.

When the Twilight of the Gods shall come, the serpent shall devour the earth and the wolf shall devour the sun.

The Panther

In medieval bestiaries, the word "Panther" refers to an animal quite different from the "carnivorous mammal" of contemporary zoology. Aristotle had said that the odor of this beast attracts other animals; Ælian, the Latin author known as the "honey-tongued" for his mastery of Greek, declared that this odor was "grateful to man," as well. (These statements have led to the conjecture that there was some confusion between the Panther and the civet cat.) According to Pliny, there are reports that "the Panther has, on the shoulder, a spot which bears the form of the moon; and that, like it, it regularly increases to full, and then diminishes to a crescent." To these marvelous circumstances there came to be added the fact that in the Septuagint, the word "Panther" is used once in a way that might refer to Christ (Hosea 5:14).

In the Anglo-Saxon bestiary known as the Exeter Book, the Panther is a solitary, kind animal with a melodious voice and a fragrant breath. It makes its home in the mountains, in a secret place. Its only enemy is the Dragon, with which it is constantly embattled. A twelfth-century Latin bestiary adds details to this description: It sleeps for three nights, and when it awakens, singing, multitudes of men and animals are drawn by the music and the fragrance of its breath, and they make their way from the fields, castles, and cities to its cave. The Dragon is the Old Enemy, the Devil; the awakening is the Resurrection of the Lord; the multitudes are the community of the faithful; and the Panther is Jesus Christ.

To mitigate the astonishment this allegory may produce, let us recall that the Panther was not a fierce and fearsome beast for the Saxons, but rather an exotic sound, backed by a none-too-concrete image. It might be added, to compound the curiosity, that Eliot's poem "Gerontion" speaks of "Christ the tiger."

Leonardo da Vinci included "the Panther in Africa" among the beasts in his *Bestiary*. Here is his description:

> This has the shape of a lioness, but it is taller in the leg and slimmer and longer and quite white, marked with black spots after the manner of rosettes; all the animals are fascinated by these as they gaze at them and they would remain standing there always if it were not for the terror of its face; being conscious of this therefore it hides its face, and the animals that are round about it take courage and draw near so as to be able the better to enjoy so much beauty: it then suddenly seizes on the nearest and instantly devours it.

The Pelican

The Pelican of ordinary zoology is an aquatic fowl approximately six feet tall with a long, broad beak from whose lower jaw there hangs a reddish membrane forming a sort of sack or basket for holding fish; the Pelican of fable is smaller, and its beak is short and sharp. Faithful to its name, the plumage of the first is white; the feathers of the second are yellow, or sometimes green. Even more striking than its appearance are its habits.

With her beak and claws, the mother bird pets her nurslings with such devotion that she kills them. Three days later, the father bird arrives; driven to desperation by finding the chicks all dead, he pecks at his own breast until he bleeds. The blood that flows from the wound brings the nurslings back to life. That is the way the bestiaries tell it, though St. Jerome, in a commentary on Psalm 102 ("I am like a pelican of the wilderness: I am like an owl of the desert"), attributes the chicks' death to the Serpent. The Pelican's tearing at its own breast and feeding its children with its own blood is the usual version of the fable.

Blood that brings life to the dead suggests, of course, the Eucharist and the Cross, and so a famous line in the *Paradiso* (XXV, 113) calls Christ "our Pelican." Benvenuto da Imola's Latin commentary makes this reference clear: "The word 'Pelican' is used because the Side was opened that we might be saved, like the Pelican that gives Life to its dead children with the Blood of its breast. The Pelican is an Egyptian bird."

The image of the Pelican is widespread in ecclesiastical heraldry, and still engraved upon chalices. Leonardo da Vinci's bestiary defines the Pelican in the following way:

This bears a great love to its young; and if it finds them slain in the nest by a serpent it pierces itself to the heart in their presence, and by bathing them with a shower of blood it restores them to life.

The Perytion

Apparently the Erithrean oracle predicted that Rome would be destroyed by the Perytions. When the sayings of that oracle disappeared (accidentally burned) in the year 642 of our era, the person responsible for restoring them failed to include that particular prediction, and therefore today there is no indication of it to be found there.

Given the obscurity of its origins, then, there was need of a source that might throw more light on the creature's habits and appearance. Thus it was that after countless difficulties the authors have learned that in the sixteenth century a rabbi in Fez (almost certainly Aaron-ben-Chaim) published a small pamphlet dedicated to fantastic animals, wherein the author mentions having read the work of a certain Arab author in which there is mentioned a treatise on the Perytions that was lost when Omar burned the library at Alexandria. Although the rabbi did not give the name of this Arab author, he did have the happy idea of transcribing a few paragraphs from his text, thereby leaving us a valuable description of the Perytion. Lacking further corroboration, we think it wise simply to reproduce those paragraphs verbatim:

> The Perytion inhabits the island of Atlantis, and is a creature half stag, half bird. It possesses the head and feet of the stag, and as for the body, it is that of a perfect bird, with all its feathers and plumage.
>
> The most astonishing feature of this beast is that when it is struck by the rays of the sun, the shadow it throws

upon the ground is not that of its own figure, but rather that of a human being; from this circumstance, some have concluded that the Perytions are the souls of men who died far from the protection of the gods. . . .

[T]hey have been come upon as they were feeding upon dry earth; . . . they fly in flocks and have been seen at high altitudes near the Pillars of Hercules.

They are fearsome enemies of mankind. It appears that if they can manage to kill a man, their shadow becomes once again that of their own body, and they attain the favor of the gods . . .

Those who crossed the seas with Scipio to conquer Carthage very nearly failed in their enterprise, for during the crossing a compact band of Perytions appeared, killing many of the sailors. . . . Although our weapons are powerless against the Perytion, the animal can kill but a single man.

They wallow in the blood of their victim and then fly off into the heavens.

In Ravenna, where they were seen not a few years ago, it is said that their feathers are sky-blue, a fact which I find most surprising, for *I have read* that the plumage is of a very dark green.

Although the foregoing paragraphs are quite specific, it is a pity that no further trustworthy information concerning the Perytion has come down to our own day. Nor has the rabbi's pamphlet from which we have taken this description managed to survive. The document could be found, until the last world war, in the library of the University of Munich. Painful to tell, the document has now disappeared, whether by consequence of the

bombardment of that city or by the work of the Nazis it is impossible to say.

It is to be hoped that if this last surmise is the real cause of its disappearance, the document will in time be found again, and added to the treasures of one of the world's great libraries.

The Phoenix

In monumental statuary, in pyramids of stone, and as mummies, the Egyptians sought eternal life; it seems only natural, then, that it should be Egypt where the myth of an immortal, periodic bird was born—though the later elaboration of the myth is the work of the Greeks and Romans. Erman writes that in the mythology of Heliopolis, the Phoenix (*benu*) is the lord of jubilees, long cycles of time; in a famous passage, Herodotus (II, 73) tells, with repeated incredulity, an early form of the legend:

> Another bird also is sacred; it is called the Phoenix. I myself have never seen it, but only pictures of it; for the bird comes but seldom into Egypt, once in five hundred years, as the people of Heliopolis say. It is said that the Phoenix comes when his father dies. If the picture truly shows his size and appearance, his plumage is partly golden but mostly red. He is most like an eagle in shape and bigness. The Egyptians tell a tale of this bird's devices which I do not believe. He comes, they say, from Arabia bringing his father the Sun's temple enclosed in myrrh, and there buries him. His manner of bringing is this: first he moulds an egg of myrrh as heavy as he can carry, and when he has proved its weight by lifting it he then hollows out the egg and puts his father in it, covering over with more myrrh the hollow in which the body lies; so the egg being with his father in it of the same weight as before, the Phoenix, after enclosing him, carries him to

the temple of the Sun in Egypt. Such is the tale of what is done by this bird.

Some five hundred years later, Tacitus and Pliny took up this marvelous story once again; Tacitus quite properly observed that antiquity is obscure, but that tradition had established the Phoenix's life span at 1,461 years (*Annals*, VI, 28). Pliny, too, researched the chronology of the Phoenix; he tells us (X, 2) that according to Manilius it lives for the space of one Platonic year, the great year or *annum magnum*. This is the time required by the sun, the moon, and the five planets to return to their original positions; Tacitus, in his *Dialogues*, claims that this "great revolution" takes 12,994 ordinary years to complete. The ancients believed that when this astronomical cycle was accomplished, universal history would be repeated down to the last detail, since the influence of the planets would be repeated: the Phoenix would, in that case, be a mirror or image of the universe. An even more precise analogy may be found in the philosophy of the Stoics, who taught that the universe dies in fire and is reborn from fire and that just as the process had no beginning, so it shall have no end.

Time has simplified the mechanism by which the Phoenix is born. Herodotus mentions an egg; Pliny, a "little worm" or maggot; but by the end of the sixth century a poem by Claudianus celebrates an immortal bird that rises again from its ashes—its own heir and a witness to the ages.

Few myths have been so widespread as that of the Phoenix. To the names of those authors already mentioned we might add Ovid (*Metamorphoses*, XV), Dante (*Inferno*, XXIV), Shakespeare (*Henry VIII*, V:4), Pellicer (*The Phoenix and Its Natural History*), Quevedo (*Parnaso español*, VI), Milton (*Samson*

Agonistes). We might also mention the Latin poem *"De Ave Phoenice,"* attributed to Lactantius, and a seventh-century Anglo-Saxon imitation of that poem. Tertullian, St. Ambrose, and Cirilus of Jerusalem have cited the Phoenix as proof of the resurrection of the flesh. Pliny mocks those physicians who prescribe remedies extracted from the nest and ashes of the Phoenix.

The Chinese Phoenix

The religious texts of the Chinese are often somewhat disappointing, for they lack the note of pathos which we have grown to expect from our own Bible. Then suddenly, in the midst of a rational passage, we come upon a moment of moving intimacy. This, for example, comes from the seventh book of Confucius's *Analects:*

> The Master said, "How I have gone downhill! It has been such a long time since I dreamt of the Duke of Chou."

And this, from the ninth book:

> The Master said, "The Phoenix does not appear nor does the River offer up its Chart. I am done for."

We are told by the commentators that the "Chart" (or sometimes "Sign") referred to in this passage is an inscription written on the back of a magic tortoise. As for the Phoenix (*Feng*), it is a bird whose plumage is of shimmering colors similar to the pheasant's or the peacock's. In prehistoric times, it would visit the gardens and palaces of virtuous emperors, the visible proof of celestial favor. The male, which had three legs, lived in the sun.

In the first century of the Christian era, the bold atheist Wang Ch'ung denied that the Phoenix was of a distinct species. He said that just as a serpent could change into a fish, and a rat change into a tortoise, and just as the stag, in times of general prosperity, was transformed into a unicorn, so the goose took the form of the Phoenix. He attributed this mutation to the "propitious liquid" which, 2,356 years before the Christian era, had made the garden of Yao, one of the exemplary emperors, grow vermilion grass. As one can see, Wang Ch'ung's information was faulty—or rather, excessive.

In the underworld there is an imaginary building called the Tower of the Phoenix.

Pygmies

The ancients believed that this race of dwarflike individuals (twenty-seven inches tall, Pliny tells us), lived within the borders of Hindustan or Ethiopia. Certain authors claim that they built their dwellings out of eggshells; others, such as Aristotle, have written that they lived under the ground, in caves. To harvest their wheat, they were said to arm themselves with axes, as though they were going forth to cut down a forest. They rode lambs and goats of a size befitting them. Each year they would be invaded by flocks of cranes that came from the steppes of Russia.

"Pygmy" was also the name of a deity whose face the Carthaginians carved on the prows of their warships, in order to terrify their enemies.

Quyata

There is an Islamic myth that speaks of the "Kuyoota" (as Lane transcribes its name): "a huge bull with four thousand eyes, and the same number of ears, noses, mouths, tongues, and feet; between every two of which was a distance of five hundred years' journey." Just as Quyata stands on the back of the fish Bahamut, on its back there stands a rock of ruby, on the rock an angel, and on the angel our own earth.

Remora

In Latin, "remora" is "delay." And that is the true intention of the word that was figuratively applied to the *Echeneis*, because it was said to hold ships stock still in their course. The process was inverted in Spanish: "*rémora*" is first the marine animal and only metaphorically the obstacle. The Remora is an ash-colored sea creature; on its ventral side, at its head, it has an oval disk whose cartilaginous ridges attach like a large suction cup to other sea animals. Pliny (IX, 41 [25]) tells us of its powers:

> There is a very small fish that is in the habit of living among the rocks, and is known as the Echeneis. It is believed that when this has attached itself to the keel of a ship its progress is impeded, and that it is from this circumstance that it takes its name. For this reason, also, it has a disgraceful repute, as being employed in love philtres, and for the purpose of retarding judgments and legal proceedings—evil properties, which are only compensated by a single merit that it possesses—it is good for staying fluxes of the womb in pregnant women, and preserves the foetus up to birth: it is never used, however, for food. Aristotle is of opinion that this fish has feet, so strong is the resemblance, by reason of the form and position of the fins. . . . Trebius Niger says that this fish is a foot in length, five fingers in thickness, and that it can retard the course of vessels; besides which, it has another peculiar property—when preserved in salt, and applied, it is able to draw up gold which has fallen into a well, however deep it may happen to be.

It is curious to see how the idea of stopping ships came to be that of slowing lawsuits and aiding pregnancies.

In another place, Pliny tells us that the Remora decided the fate of the Roman Empire:

> At the battle of Actium, it is said, a fish of this kind stopped the prætorian ship of Antonius in its course, at the moment he was hastening from his ship to encourage and exhort his men. . . . [And in] our own time, too, one of these fish arrested the ship of the Emperor Caius [Caligula] in its course, when he was returning from Astura to Antium.

"Winds may blow," Pliny says, "and storms may rage, and yet the Echeneis controls their fury, restrains their mighty force, and bids ships stand still in their career; a result which no cables, no anchors, from their ponderousness quite incapable of being weighed, could ever have produced!"

"It is not always the greatest might that conquers," Diego de Saavedra Fajardo repeats, in his *Empresas políticas*, "when the course of a ship may be halted by the small Remora."

A Reptile Dreamed by C. S. Lewis

Slowly, shakily, with unnatural and inhuman movements a human form, scarlet in the firelight, crawled out on to the floor of the cave. It was the Un-man, of course: dragging its broken leg and with its lower jaw sagging open like that of a corpse, it raised itself to a standing position. And then, close behind it, something else came up out of the hole. First came what looked like branches of trees, and then seven or eight spots of light, irregularly grouped like a constellation. Then a tubular mass which reflected the red glow as if it were polished. His heart gave a great leap as the branches suddenly resolved themselves into long wiry feelers and the dotted lights became the many eyes of a shell-helmeted head and the mass that followed it was revealed as a large roughly cylindrical body. Horrible things followed—angular, many jointed legs, and presently, when he thought the whole body was in sight, a second body came following it and after that a third. The thing was in three parts, united only by a kind of wasp's waist structure—three parts that did not seem to be truly aligned and made it look as if it had been trodden on—a huge, many legged, quivering deformity, standing just behind the Un-man so that the horrible shadows of both danced in enormous and united menace on the wall of rock behind them.

—C. S. Lewis, *Perelandra*

The Roc

The Roc (or *rukh*) is a magnification of the eagle or the vulture, and there are those who believe that a condor, straying into the seas of China or Hindustan, suggested the existence of such a bird to the Arabs. Lane, however, rejects this conjecture: in his view, it is more likely to be a fabulous species of a fabulous genus, or perhaps the Arabic synonym for the Simurgh. The Roc owes its Western fame to the *Arabian Nights*. Our readers will recall that Sindbad, left behind by his shipmates on an island, saw, far off in the distance, an enormous white dome; the next day, a vast cloud hid the sun. The dome was the egg of the bird known as the Roc and the cloud was the mother bird returning to it. Sindbad used his turban to tie himself to the Roc's huge claw; the bird flew up and left Sindbad upon the pinnacle of a mountain without ever having noticed him. The narrator adds that the Roc feeds its chicks with elephants.

In Marco Polo's *Travels* (III,36), we read:

> 'Tis said that in those other Islands to the south, which the ships are unable to visit because this strong current prevents their return, is found the bird *Gryphon*, which appears there at certain seasons. The description given of it is however entirely different from what our stories and pictures make it. For persons who had been there and had seen it told Messer Marco Polo that it was for all the world like an eagle, but one indeed of enormous size; so big in fact that its wings covered an extent of 30 paces, and its quills were 12 paces long, and thick in proportion. And it is so strong that it will seize an elephant in its talons

and carry him high into the air, and drop him so that he is smashed to pieces; having so killed him the bird Gryphon swoops down on him and eats him at leisure. The people of those isles call the bird *Ruc,* and it has no other name. So I wot not if this be the real Gryphon, or if there be another manner of bird as great. But this I can tell you for certain, that they are not half lion and half bird as our stories do relate; but enormous as they be they are fashioned just like an Eagle.

Marco Polo adds that emissaries sent out by the Great Khan to those southerly islands brought back to him "a feather of the said Ruc, which was stated to measure 90 spans, whilst the quill part was two palms in circumference, a marvellous object!"

The Salamander

The Salamander is not just a small dragon that lives in fire; it is also (if the dictionary is to be believed) "any of numerous amphibians (order *Caudata*) superficially resembling lizards but scaleless and covered with a soft moist skin and breathing by gills in the larval stage." (In an important Spanish-language dictionary, there are two added details: the Salamander is "insectivorous," and it is dark black with symmetrical yellow spots.) Of these characterizations, the best known is the one of fable, and no one should be surprised to find it included in this volume.

In the tenth volume of his *Natural History*, Pliny says that this animal "is so intensely cold as to extinguish fire by its contact, in the same way as ice does," but in Book XXIX he reconsiders, observing incredulously that "as to what the magicians say, that it . . . has the property of extinguishing fire, if it had been true, it would have been made trial of at Rome long before this."

In Book XI, Pliny speaks of a "four-footed animal with wings" which lives "in the copper-smelting furnaces of Cyprus, in the very midst of fire." This is the Pyrausta. "So long as it remains in the fire," says Pliny, "it will live, but if it comes out and flies a little distance from it, it will instantly die." The later myth of the Salamander incorporates much of the myth of this other, forgotten creature.

The Pheonix was often cited by theologians in order to prove the resurrection of the body; the Salamander, as proof that bodies could live in fire. In the twenty-first book of St. Augustine's *City of God*, one chapter is titled "Whether bodies can survive in a burning fire," and in that chapter we read the following:

What proof then can I offer to convince unbelievers that it is possible for human bodies, endowed with soul and life, not merely never to be decomposed by death, but also to outlast the torments of eternal flames? They refuse to accept from us an appeal to the power of the Almighty, but press us to cite a precedent by way of argument. We can reply that there are animals, which are certainly liable to destruction, since they are mortal, but still survive in the midst of flames.

The example of Salamanders and Phoenixes is also employed by poets, for rhetorical emphasis. Thus, Quevedo, in the sonnets of Book IV of his *Parnaso español*, which treats of "feats of love and of loveliness," writes as follows:

> *Hago verdad al Fénix en la ardiente*
> *Llama, en que renaciendo me renuevo,*
> *Y la virilidad del fuego pruebo*
> *Y que es padre, y que tiene descendiente:*

> *La Salamandra fría, que desmiente*
> *Noticia docta, a defender me atrevo,*
> *Cuando en incendios, que sediento bebo*
> *Mi corazón habita, y no los siente*

These lines might be translated as follows:

> In me thou mayst see the Phoenix in the burning flame,
> For, reviving, I am renewed,
> And the virility of the fire I prove—
> The bird that's father and offspring the same.

The Salamander cold, which to learnèd wisdom
Gives the lie—defend the beast I dare;
For in th' flames to which I thirsty repair,
My heart doth live, nor is ever burnt by them.

Toward the middle of the twelfth century, a false letter circulated throughout the nations of Europe, supposedly sent by Prester John, the king of kings, to the emperor of the Byzantine Empire. This epistle, which was a catalog of wonders, speaks of monstrous ants that dig for gold; of a River of Stones; of a Sea of Sand in which there swim live fishes; of a lofty mirror that reveals all that happens in the kingdom; of a scepter carved from a single emerald; and of pebbles that make a man invisible or light up the night. One of the paragraphs in that letter runs as follows: "Our dominions produce the worm known as Salamander. Salamanders live in fire and make cocoons, which the ladies of the palace unwind and use for weaving cloth and making clothing. In order to wash and clean this cloth, it is thrown into the fire."

One may also find mention of this incombustible fabric that is washed in fire in Pliny (XIX, 4) and in Marco Polo, who says that we "must understand that this is not a beast as is commonly asserted; but its real nature is [a substance]." No one at first believed Marco Polo; the cloth, woven from asbestos, was sold as Salamander skin and served as incontrovertible proof that the Salamander existed.

Early in his *Life,* Benvenuto Cellini tells the following story:

When I was about five years old my father happened to be in a basement-chamber of our house, where they had been washing, and where a good fire of oak-logs was still burning. . . . Happening to look into the fire, he spied in the middle of those most burning flames a little creature like a lizard, which was sporting in the core of the intensest coals. Becoming instantly aware of what the thing was, he had my sister and me called, and pointing it out to us children, gave me a great box on the ears, which caused me to howl and weep with all my might. Then he pacified me good-humouredly, and spoke as follows: "My dear little boy, I am not striking you for any wrong that you have done, but only to make you remember that that lizard which you see in the fire is a salamander, a creature which has never been seen before by any one of whom we have credible information."

In the symbology of alchemy, Salamanders are the elementary spirits of the fire. It is in that attribution, and in an argument by Aristotle that Cicero has preserved for us in the first book of his *De natura Deorum*, that we discover why men so often believe in the Salamander. The Sicilian physician Empedocles of Agrigentum had formulated a theory of the "four roots of things," whose joinings and disjoinings, moved by Love and Discord, made universal history. There was no death; there were only the particles of these "roots," which the Romans called "elements," coming apart. The roots are fire, earth, air, and water. They are uncreated elements, and none is stronger than any other. We now know (we now *think* we know) that this doctrine is not true, but mankind thought it beautiful, and it is generally admitted that the theory was at least helpful in some ways. "The four elements that compose and maintain the world, and which still survive in poetry and in the popular imagination, have a long and glorious history," Theodor Gomperz wrote. The doctrine required that there be a certain equality among the four elements: If there were animals of land and of water, then there had to be animals of fire. It was necessary for the dignity of science, therefore, that there be Salamanders. In another place, we find that Aristotle managed to conceive animals of air.

Leonardo da Vinci believed that the Salamander nourished itself on fire, and that it used fire to help it shed its skin.

Satyrs

That was the name by which the Greeks called them; in Rome, they were called Fauns, Pans, and Sylvani. From the waist down they were goats; their bodies, arms, and faces were human, though hairy. They had pointed ears, a hooked nose, and little horns on their foreheads. They were lustful, drunken creatures that accompanied the god Bacchus in his merry conquest of Hindustan. They often lay in wait to pounce upon unsuspecting Nymphs; they loved to dance; and they were skillful players of the flute. Peasants venerated them, and made offerings to them of the first fruits of their harvests; they also sacrificed lambs to them.

Legend has it that one of these minor deities was captured in a cave in Thessaly by the men of one of Sulla's legions, and taken to the general. It made inarticulate sounds and was so repulsive that Sulla immediately ordered that it be returned to its mountain lair.

The memory of the Satyrs influenced the medieval image of the devil.

Scylla

Before she was a monster and a whirlpool, Scylla was a nymph with whom the god Glaucus fell in love. Spurned by the nymph, Glaucus sought the help of Circe, famed for her knowledge of herbs and magic spells. Circe became enamored of Glaucus, but when Glaucus refused to renounce his love for Scylla, Circe poisoned the waters in the cove where the nymph was wont to bathe. At first contact with the water, the lower part of Scylla's body turned into barking dogs—twelve feet and six heads, each head with two rows of sharp teeth, were now her nether parts. This metamorphosis terrified her, and she threw herself into the strait between Italy and Sicily, where the gods changed her into a rock. During storms, sailors can still hear the howling of the waves against that rock.

This fable is told in the pages of Homer, Ovid, and Pausanias.

The Sea Horse

Unlike other fantastic animals, the Sea Horse was not conceived as a combination of heterogeneous elements; it is simply a wild stallion that lives in the sea and emerges onto dry land only when the breeze brings it the scent of mares on moonless nights. On an unspecified island—Borneo, perhaps—the king's grooms picket the king's finest mares along the seashore and then hide themselves in underground chambers. Sindbad saw the young horse that came up out of the sea, he saw it mount the female and heard its whinny.

The definitive collection of the *Book of the Thousand and One Nights* dates, Burton says, from the thirteenth century; it was in the thirteenth century, too, that the cosmographer Al-Qazwini lived and died. In his treatise *The Wonders of Creation*, Al-Qazwini wrote these words: "The Sea Horse is like unto the horse of the land, but its mane and tail are longer and its color more lustrous and its hoof cleft like that of wild oxen; it does not stand so tall as the horse of the land, although it is somewhat taller than the ass." He remarks that the hybrid that results when the sea species mates with the terrestrial species is very beautiful, and he mentions a dark colt "with white spots like pieces of silver."

In the *Chinese Miscellany*, Wang Tai-hai, a thirteenth-century traveler, wrote the following words:

The Sea Horse frequently comes on shore to seek after its mate; on which occasions it is sometimes caught. Its hair is of a fine black colour and very sleek; its tail is long and sweeps the ground; on shore it walks about like other horses, is very tractable, and will go several hundred miles in a day; but you must not attempt to bathe it in the river; for no sooner does it see water, than its former nature revives, and darting into the stream, it swims away; and as its strength is great it is not to be caught again.

Ethnologists have sought the origin of this Islamic fantasy in the Greco-Latin fiction of the wind by which mares are inseminated. In the third book of the *Georgics*, Virgil described this belief. Pliny's description is more rigorous (VIII, 67):

It is well known that in Lusitania, in the vicinity of the town of Olisipo (now Lisbon) and the river Tagus, the mares, by turning their faces towards the west wind as it blows, become impregnated by its breezes, and that the foals that are conceived in this way are remarkable for their extreme fleetness; but they never live beyond three years.

The historian Justinus has conjectured that the hyperbole "progeny of the wind," applied to swift horses, was the origin of this fable.

The Eight-Forked-Serpent

The Eight-Forked-Serpent-of-Koshi, the "man-devourer," is a fearful beast in Japanese cosmogonic myths. "Its eyes are red as the winter-cherry, its body is single, eight-headed and eight-tailed, rock firs grow on each of its heads, on each of its sides is a mountain, and on its back grow moss, pine-trees and cryptomeria. Its length, as it crawls, trails over eight valleys and eight hills, and its belly to the sight is always bloody and fomented." This monster had devoured seven maidens, the daughters of a king, over a period of seven years, and it was preparing to devour the eighth, the youngest, named Princess-Comb-Ricefield, when she was saved by a deity figure named Brave-Swift-Impetuous-Male. This knight *avant la lettre* counseled the king to "build a circular fence, and in the fence to make eight gates, and at the gates to tie eight platforms, and on each platform to set a liquor tub and in each tub to pour an eightfold refined poisonous spirit, a strong rice beer, and then to await the serpent's coming. When the Eight-Forked-Serpent came, it found the spirit, dipped a head into each of the tubs and drank, and becoming drunken, laid down all its heads and slept. At that, Brave-Swift-Impetuous-Male, drawing his ten-hand-lengths sword, severed its heads and belly." From the wounds, we are told, there flowed a river of blood, and within the flesh of the serpent's tail Brave-Swift-Impetuous-Male found a sword, now called Herb-Queller, which is still worshipped at the Great Sanctuary of At-suta. These things occurred on the mountain previously called Serpent's-Mountain and now called Eight-Cloud Mountain; in Japan the number eight is sacred, and signifies "many." To this day the paper money of Japan commemorates the death of Eight-Forked-Serpent.

It is surely unnecessary to add that the victor married the rescued maiden, as Perseus married Andromeda.

In his English version of the cosmogonies and theogonies of old Japan (*The Sacred Scriptures of the Japanese*, New York, 1952), Post Wheeler recalls, among others, the analogous myths of the Hydra, the Fafnir, and the Egyptian goddess Hathor, "who was made drunk from blood-red beer poured from jars so that she would cease from slaying mankind."

The Simurgh

The Simurgh is an immortal bird that makes its nest in the branches of the Tree of Science; Burton equates it with the Norse eagle that the Younger Edda tells us has knowledge of many things and builds its nest in the branches of the World-Tree, Yggdrasil.

Southey's *Thalaba* (1801) and Flaubert's *The Temptation of St. Anthony* mention the Simorg Anka. Flaubert reduces the bird to a sort of attendant upon the Queen of Sheba, and describes it in this way: "Its orange-colored plumage seems formed of metallic scales. Its little head, crested with a silver tuft, has a human face. It has four wings, the feet of a vulture, and an immense peacock's tail which it spreads open like a fan." In the original sources, the Simurgh is much less colorful, but much more important. Firdusi, in his *Book of Kings*, which is a compilation and versification of ancient Irani legends, makes him the adoptive father of Zal, the father of the poem's hero. The thirteenth-century poet Farīd al-dīn Abī Ḥamīd Muḥammad ben Ibrāhīm (called 'Aṭṭar or "perfumer"), in his mystical epic *Manṭiq al-ṭair* ("The Language [or 'Colloquy' or perhaps 'Parliament'] of the Birds"), elevates the bird into a symbol or image of the deity. The plot of this allegory, which is composed of some four thousand five hundred couplets, is curious: One of the splendid feathers of the distant King of the Birds, the Simurgh, falls into the center of China; other birds, weary with the present state of anarchy, resolve to find this king. They know that the name of their king means "thirty birds"; they know that his palace is in the Mountains of Kaf, the mountains that encircle the earth. At the beginning, some of the birds reconsider their rashness, and grow cowardly: the nightingale excuses itself from the journey-quest because of its love for the rose; the parrot, because of its beauty, which is the reason it lives within a cage; the partridge says it cannot live without the high mountains, while the heron pleads its need for the marshes, the owl, for ruins. But at last the birds undertake the desperate quest. They cross seven *wadis* or seven seas. The penultimate of these is called Vertigo; the last, Annihilation. Many pilgrims abandon the quest; others perish on the journey. At the end, thirty birds, purified by their travails, come to the mountain on which the Simurgh lives, and they contemplate their king at last: they see that they are the Simurgh, and that the Simurgh is each of them, and all of them.

The cosmographer Al-Qazwini, in his *Wonders of the Creation*, tells us that the Simurgh 'Anqa lives for one thousand seven hundred years, and when its son is grown the father lights a pyre and immolates himself. "This," Lane observes, "recalls the legend of the Phoenix."

Sirens

Through the centuries, the Sirens' shape has changed. The first historian of these creatures, the rhapsodist of *The Odyssey* (Book XII), does not describe them; Ovid tells us they are birds with golden plumage and the face of a virgin. For Apollonius of Rhodes, the top half of their body is a woman's and the bottom, a seabird's; for Tirso de Molina (and for heraldry), they are half fish, half woman. Nor is their nature any less disputed: Lemprière's dictionary says that they are nymphs, while Quicherat's says they are monsters and Grimal's, demons. They inhabit one of the Western Isles, near the island of Circe, but the body of one Siren, Parthenope, was found in the Campagna. She gave her name to the famous city that we now know as Naples; the geographer Strabo saw her tomb and witnessed the gymnastic games that are periodically held in her memory.

The Odyssey says that the Sirens' singing would lure sailors to shipwreck and death by drowning, and that in order to hear the Sirens' song and yet not perish, Ulysses commanded his rowers to stop their ears with beeswax and tie him to the mast. The Sirens tempted the warrior with the knowledge of all things on earth:

> Sea rovers here take joy
> Voyaging onward,
> As from our song of Troy
> Greybeard and rower-boy
> Goeth more learned.
>
> All feats on that great field
> In the long warfare,

Dark days the bright gods willed,
  Wounds you bore there,

Argos' old soldiery
  On Troy beach teeming,
Charmed out of time we see.
No life on earth can be
  Hid from our dreaming.

A legend contained in the *Library* of the mythologer Apollodorus tells that Orpheus, in the Argonaut's ship, sang sweeter than the Sirens, and that upon hearing him, the Sirens threw themselves into the sea where they were transformed into rocks, for they were fated to die whenever a man did not fall under their spell. (The Sphinx also threw itself from a mountaintop when its riddle was guessed.)

Sometime in the sixth century, a Siren was captured in the north of Wales and baptized, and even listed as a saint in certain ancient calendars, under the name Murgen. Another came through a break in a dike in 1403, and lived in Haarlem until her death. No one could understand her, but she taught people to spin and she worshipped the cross, as though instinctively. A sixteenth-century chronicler reasoned that she was not a fish, for she knew how to spin, nor yet was she a woman, for she could live in water.

The English language makes a distinction between the classical Siren and that creature with a fish's tail that is called a Mermaid. It was no doubt an analogy with the Tritons, deities in the court of Poseidon, that influenced the shape of these latter creatures.

In the tenth book of the *Republic,* eight Sirens preside over the revolution of the eight concentric spheres of the heavens.

"Siren: an imaginary marine animal," we read in one particularly uncouth dictionary.

The Sow in Chains

On page 106 of the *Dictionary of Argentine Folklore* (Buenos Aires, 1950), Félix Colluccio includes the following description:

In northern Córdoba, and especially around Quilinos, people talk of a Sow in Chains; this animal generally makes its appearance during the hours of night. The people who live near the train station say that the Sow in Chains sometimes glides along the tracks, while others have told us that it is not unusual for it to run along the telegraph lines, making an infernal noise with its chains. No one has been able to see it, since when one goes out looking for it, it mysteriously disappears.

The Sphinx

The Sphinx found on Egyptian monuments (called "Androsphinx" by Herodotus, to distinguish it from the Greek creature) is a recumbent lion with the head of a man; it is believed to represent the authority of the pharaoh, and it guarded the tombs and temples of that land. Other Sphinxes, on the avenues of Karnak, have the head of a lamb, the animal sacred to Amon. Bearded and crowned Sphinxes are found on monuments in Assyria, and it is a common image on Persian jewelry. Pliny includes Sphinxes in his catalog of Ethiopian animals, but the only description he offers is that it has "brown hair and two mammae on the breast."

The Greek Sphinx has the head and breasts of a woman, the wings of a bird, and the body and legs of a lion. Others give it the body of a dog and the tail of a serpent. Legend recounts that it devastated the countryside of Thebes by demanding that travelers on the roads solve riddles that it put to them (it had a human voice); it devoured those who could not answer. This was the famous question it put to Oedipus, son of Jocasta: "What has four feet, two feet, or three feet, and the more feet it has, the weaker it is?"*

Oedipus answered that it was man, who crawls on four legs as a child, walks upon two legs as a man, and leans upon a stick in old age. The Sphinx, its riddle solved, leapt to its death from a mountaintop.

*This is apparently the oldest version of the riddle. The years have added the metaphor of the life of man as a single day, so that we now know the following version of it: "What animal walks on four legs in the morning, two legs at midday, and three in the evening?"

In 1849 Thomas De Quincey suggested a second interpretation, which might complement the traditional one. The answer to the riddle, according to De Quincey, is less man in general than Oedipus himself, a helpless orphan in his morning, alone in the fullness of his manhood, and leaning upon Antigone in his blind and hopeless old age.

The Squonk

(Lacrimacorpus dissolvens)

The range of the Squonk is very limited. Few people outside of Pennsylvania have ever heard of the quaint beast, which is said to be fairly common in the hemlock forests of that state. The Squonk is of a very retiring disposition, generally traveling about at twilight and dusk. Because of its misfitting skin, which is covered with warts and moles, it is always unhappy; in fact it is said, by people who are best able to judge, to be the most morbid of beasts. Hunters who are good at tracking are able to follow a Squonk by its tear-stained trail, for the animal weeps constantly. When cornered and escape seems impossible, or when surprised and frightened, it may even dissolve itself in tears. Squonk hunters are most successful on frosty moonlight nights, when tears are shed slowly and the animal dislikes moving about; it may then be heard weeping under the boughs of dark hemlock trees. Mr. J. P. Wentling, formerly of Pennsylvania, but now at St. Anthony Park, Minnesota, had a disappointing experience with a Squonk near Mont Alto. He made a clever capture by mimicking the Squonk and inducing it to hop into a sack, in which he was carrying it home, when suddenly the burden lightened and the weeping ceased. Wentling unslung the sack and looked in. There was nothing but tears and bubbles.

—William T. Cox, *Fearsome Creatures of the Lumberwoods,*
With a Few Desert and Mountain Beasts

The Celestial Stag

We know nothing of the shape of the Celestial Stag (perhaps because no one has ever clearly seen one), but we do know that these tragic animals live underground and wish for nothing but to come out into the light of day. They possess the power of speech, and they plead with miners to help them escape. At first they try to bribe them with the promise of precious ores; when this stratagem fails, the Stags insult and vex the miners, who overpower the animals and immure them within the mine. It is also said that the Stags sometimes torment men and cause their death.

Tradition adds that if the Stags do emerge into the light, they become a foul-smelling liquid that "deals pestilence and death around."

This fiction is Chinese, and may be read in the book titled *Chinese Ghouls and Goblins* (London, 1928) by G. Willoughby-Meade.

Sylphs

For each of the four roots or elements into which the Greeks divided matter there was a corresponding spirit. In the work of Paracelsus, the sixteenth-century Swiss alchemist and physician, we find four elementary spirits: the Gnomes of earth, the Nymphs of water, the Salamanders of fire, and the Sylphs or Sylphides of air. These words are of Greek origin. Littré has sought the etymology of "sylph" in the Celtic tongues, but it is most unlikely that Paracelsus would have known, or even suspected the existence of, those languages.

Today, no one believes in Sylphs, but the phrase "a sylphlike figure" is still applied to slender women, as a somewhat clichéd compliment. The Sylphs occupy a place between that of material beings and that of immaterial beings. Romantic poetry and the ballet find them useful.

Talos

Living creatures made of stone or metal constitute an alarming species within fantastic zoology. We might recall the fire-breathing bronze bulls that Jason, with the aid of Medea's magic, yoked to the plow; Condillac's statue of sentient marble endowed with a human psyche; and, in the *Thousand Nights and a Night*, the man of gleaming metal, wearing a leaden plate upon his breast inscribed with mystic signs and talismans, who rescued and then abandoned the third Kalandar when the Kalandar toppled the brass horseman that stood atop the Lodestone Mountain. Other such creatures are the "girls of mild silver, or of furious gold" that a goddess in the mythology of William Blake snared in nets of silk for a man; the metallic birds that were the nursemaids of Ares; and Talos, who guarded the isle of Crete.* Some declare Talos to be the work of Vulcan or of Dædalus; Apollonius of Rhodes, in the *Argonautica*, says that he was the last survivor of the Race of Brass.

Three times each day Talos circled Crete, hurling boulders at those who attempted to disembark. Heated red hot, he embraced men and killed them. His only vulnerable spot was his heel; instructed by the sorceress Medea, Castor and Pollux—the Dioscuri—slew him.

---

*To this catalog we might add a draft animal: the swift wild boar Guillinbursti, whose name means "he of the golden sows," and which was also called Slidrugtanni, "he of the dangerous tusks." "This living creature of ironwork," writes the mythologer Paul Herrmann, "emerged from the forge of the skillful dwarves, who threw into the fire a pigskin and withdrew a golden boar, able to run on land, in water, and through the air. However dark the night may be, there is always sufficient light in that place where the golden boar is found." Guillinbursti pulls the chariot of Freyr, the Norse god of generation and fertility.

The T'ao-T'ieh

The existence of this creature is unknown to poets and mythology alike, but all of us, at one time or another, have come upon it, in the corner of a capital or the center of a frieze, and have felt a slight shudder of revulsion. Orthrus, the dog that guarded the cattle of the three-bodied Geryon (and that Hercules quickly dispatched), had two heads and one body; the T'ao T'ieh inverts this image, and is even more horrible, for its huge head is attached to one body on the right and another on the left. It generally has six legs, since its forelegs serve both bodies. Its head may be that of a dragon, a tiger, or a person; historians of art call it the "ogre-mask." It is a monster of form, inspired by the devil of symmetry in the imagination of sculptors, potters, and ceramicists. Fourteen hundred years before the Christian era, during the Shang dynasty, it already figured on ritual bronzes.

"T'ao-T'ieh" means "glutton." The Chinese paint it on porcelains in order to "warn against self-indulgence."

194

Thermal Beings

The visionary theosophist Rudolf Steiner experienced a revelation through which he learned that this planet, before it became the Earth that we know, passed through three stages, or incarnations: the first was that of Saturn, then that of the Sun, and then that of the Moon. The human being is, at the present time, composed of four members: the physical body, the life body (or ethereal body), the astral body, and the ego; at the beginning of the Saturn stage of evolution it was a physical body alone. But this body was neither visible nor tangible, since at that time there were neither solids nor liquids nor gases on the earth; there was a state "only of 'heat.'"—Thermal Forms. Various colors defined the regular and irregular forms that inhabited cosmic space; each man, each being, was an organism whose "matter" was changing temperatures. According to Steiner, the human beings of the Saturn era were a deaf and dumb and impalpable complex of articulated colds and heats. His *Geheimwissenschaft im Umriß* ("Outline of the Occult Sciences") tells us that "for the researcher, heat is only a substance still finer than gas." Before the Sun stage of evolution, archangels, or spirits of fire, animated the bodies of these "human beings," who began to shine and glow.

Did Rudolf Steiner dream these things? Did he dream them because they had actually occurred, far back in the depths of time? One thing we do know—they are much more awe-inspiring than the demiurges and serpents and bulls of other cosmogonies.

The Tigers of Annam

For the people of Annam, Tigers (or spirits personified by Tigers) rule the four directions:

The Red Tiger rules the south (which is at the top of maps); it is the Tiger of summer and fire.

The Black Tiger rules the north; it is the Tiger of winter and water.

The Blue Tiger rules the east; it is the Tiger of spring and plants.

The White Tiger rules the west; it is the Tiger of fall and metals.

Above these four Cardinal Tigers there is another Tiger, the Yellow Tiger, which rules the others and is in the center, as the emperor is in the center of China and China is in the center of the world. (This is why China is called the Middle Kingdom, and why it occupies the center of the map of the world that Father Ricci, of the Company of Jesus, drew in the late sixteenth century in order to illuminate the Chinese.)

Lao-Tse charges the Five Tigers with the mission of battling demons. One Annamite prayer, translated into French by Louis Cho Chod, implores the aid of the Tigers' impregnable armies. This superstition is of Chinese origin; Sinologists tell us of a White Tiger that rules over the remote lands of the western stars. In the south, the Chinese set a Red Bird; in the east, a Blue Dragon; in the north, a Black Tortoise. As we see, the Annamites have preserved the colors, but have reduced the animals to one.

The Bhils, a people in central Hindustan, believe in hells for Tigers; the Malays know of a city in the heart of the jungle, with roofbeams of human bones, walls of human skin, and thatch of human hair, that was built and lived in by Tigers.

Trolls

In England the Valkyries came to be relegated to villages, where they degenerated into witches; in the Scandinavian countries the giants of ancient mythology, who lived in Jotunheim and battled against the god Thor, have degenerated into rustic Trolls. In the cosmography that fills the Elder Edda, we read that on the day of the Twilight of the Gods the giants scaled Bifrost, the rainbow bridge, and tore it down and, aided by a wolf and a serpent, destroyed the world; the Trolls of popular superstition are evil, stupid elves that dwell in mountain caves or in rundown huts. The most distinguished among them have two or three heads.

Henrik Ibsen's dramatic poem *Peer Gynt* (1867) has assured their fame. Ibsen imagines that they are first and foremost nationalists; they think, or attempt to think, that the horrid drink they brew is delicious and that their caves are palaces. To prevent Peer Gynt from seeing how sordid their dwelling places are, they threaten to put out his eyes.

The Unicorn

The first and last versions of the Unicorn are virtually identical. Four centuries before the Christian era, the Greek author Ctesias, physician to Artaxerxes Mnemon, reported that in the kingdoms of Hindustan there were extremely swift wild asses, with white skin, a purple head, blue eyes, and a sharp horn on the forehead; the base of this horn, Ctesias tells us, was white, its tip was red, and in the middle it was thoroughly black. Pliny (VIII, 31) gives yet more detail:

> The Orsæan Indians hunt down . . . a very fierce animal called the Monoceros, which has the head of the stag, the feet of the elephant, and the tail of the boar, while the rest of the body is like that of the horse; it makes a deep lowing noise, and has a single black horn, which projects from the middle of its forehead, two cubits in length. This animal, it is said, cannot be taken alive.

In 1892 the Orientalist Schrader posited that the Unicorn might have been suggested to the Greeks by certain Persian bas reliefs portraying bulls in profile, so that only one horn was shown.

In the *Etymologies* of Isidore of Seville (composed in the early seventh century), we read that a blow from the horn of the Unicorn can kill an elephant; this recalls the analogous victory of the Karkadan (rhinoceros) in the second voyage of Sindbad.* An-

---

*Sindbad tells us that the rhinoceros's horn, "when cleft in twain, is the likeness of a man"; Al-Qazwini says it is the figure of a man on horseback, and others mention birds and fishes.

other of the Unicorn's adversaries was the lion, and one of the nine-line "Spenserians" in the second book of that tangled allegory *The Faërie Queene* has preserved the way a battle between those two noble creatures might be fought: The lion would stand in front of a tree; the Unicorn, head lowered, charges; the lion steps aside, and the Unicorn's horn sticks in the tree trunk. This description dates from the sixteenth century; at the beginning of the eighteenth, the union between England and Scotland would pit the English Leopard (or Lion) against the Scottish Unicorn on the kingdoms' coats of arms.

In the Middle Ages, bestiaries taught that the Unicorn might be captured by a virgin; in the *Physiologus Græcus,* we read the following: "He can be trapped by the following strategem: A virgin girl is led to where he lurks, and there she is sent off by herself into the wood. He soon leaps into her lap when he sees her, and embraces her, and hence he gets caught." A medallion by Pisanello and many famous tapestries illustrate this victory, whose allegorical applications are familiar to us all. The Holy Spirit, Christ, mercury, and evil have been symbolized at one time or another by the Unicorn. Jung's treatise *Psychologie und Alchemie* (Zurich, 1944) records and analyzes these symbols.

A little white horse with the forelegs of an antelope, the beard of a goat, and a long twisted horn on its forehead is today the most common image of this fantastic animal.

Leonardo da Vinci attributes the Unicorn's capture to the beast's "lack of temperance" and "the delight that it has for young maidens"; that aspect of its nature makes it "forget its ferocity and wildness" and lie in the lap of the maiden, and thus it is captured by hunters.

The Chinese Unicorn

The Chinese Unicorn, or K'i-Lin, is one of the four animals of good omen; the others are the Dragon, the Phoenix, and the Tortoise. The Unicorn is the foremost of the four-legged animals; it has the body of a Kiun (or deer), the tail of an ox, and the hoofs of a horse; the horn that grows from its forehead is fleshy. Its back is of five mingled colors; its underside is brown or yellow. It will not tread upon green grass or do harm to any creature. Its appearance is said to be auspicious, and to augur the birth of a virtuous ruler. It is bad luck to wound it or to find the body of a dead K'i-Lin. Its natural lifespan is a thousand years.

When Confucius' mother was carrying him within her womb, the spirits of the five planets brought her an animal "with the shape of a cow, the scales of a dragon, and a horn in its forehead." That is one version of the annunciation; a variant collected by Legge says that the animal came of its own accord and spat out a jade plaque on which were written the following words:

> Son of the mountain crystal [that is, the essence of water], when the dynasty has fallen, thou shalt rule like a king without royal insignias.

Some seventy years later, hunters killed a K'i-Lin whose horn still bore a piece of the ribbon that Confucius' mother had tied there. Confucius went to see it, and he wept, for he sensed what the death of that innocent, mysterious animal meant and also because within that ribbon lay the past.

In the thirteenth century, Marco Polo tells us, Genghis Khan waged a campaign against India, and accompanying him was the celebrated minister Yeh-lü Ch'u-ts'ai. In the Kara Dagh region the expedition met a creature "like a deer, with a head like that of a horse, one horn on its forehead, and green hair on its body." The creature addressed the guards, saying, "It is time for your master to return to his own land." When the Great Khan consulted Yeh-lü Ch'u-ts'ai, the minister replied: "That creature is the Chio-tuan (a variety of the K'i-Lin). It appears as a sign that bloodshed is needless at present. For four years the great army has been warring in Western regions. Heaven, which has a horror of bloodshed, gives warning through the Chio-tuan." The emperor thereupon desisted from his bellicose designs.

Twenty-two centuries before the Christian era, one of the judges of the emperor Shun possessed a "one-horned goat" that "knew the innocent from the guilty. It would butt the guilty with its single horn, but refused to attack those wrongly accused."

In his *Anthologie raisonnée de la littérature chinoise* (1948), Margouliès includes this calm yet mysterious fable, from the pen of a ninth-century author:

> It is universally acknowledged that the Unicorn is a su-
> pernatural creature of good omen; thus declare the odes,
> the annals, the biographies of worthy men, and other texts
> whose authority is beyond question. Even the women of
> the villages and young children know that the Unicorn is
> a favorable sign. But this animal does not figure among
> the domestic animals, nor may one find it in the world;
> nor does its shape lend itself to classification. It is not like
> the horse or the bull, the dog or the pig, the wolf or

the deer. In such circumstances, even if one stood in the presence of a Unicorn, it would be hard to be certain that it is one. We know that a certain animal with a mane is a horse and that a certain animal with horns is a bull. We know the appearances of dogs, pigs, wolves, and deer. We do not know the shape of the Unicorn.

Valkyries

In the primitive Germanic tongues, "valkyrie" means "she who chooses the dead." An Anglo-Saxon spell against muscle pain describes such a creature, without naming her directly, in the following way:

> Resonant were they, yea, resonant, when riding on high,
> And resolute, when they rode over the earth,
> Powerful women.

We cannot be certain how the peoples of Germany or Austria conceived them; in Scandinavian mythology they are beautiful, armed virgins. They were generally thought to be three in number.

The Valkyries chose those who had died in combat and carried their souls up to Odin's epic paradise, where the roof was of gold and illumination came from swords, not lamps. Beginning at dawn, the warriors of that paradise would battle until they died, when they would come to life again and sit down at the banquet of the gods, where they would be served the flesh of an immortal boar and inexhaustible horns of mead.

Under the growing influence of Christianity, the reputation of the Valkyries declined; a judge in medieval England ordered a woman accused of being a Valkyrie—a witch, that is—burned.

Youwarkee

In his *Short History of English Literature*, Saintsbury says that in his opinion, Youwarkee is one of the most delightful heroines of that literature. This creature was half woman and half bird, or (as Robert Browning wrote of his dead wife Elizabeth Barrett) half angel and half bird. Her arms opened into wings, and a silky plumage covered her body. She dwelt on a deserted island in the Antarctic seas; there, she was discovered by a shipwrecked sailor, Peter Wilkins, who took her as his wife. Youwarkee is of the race of Glums, a winged tribe. Wilkins converts her to Christianity; when his wife dies, he manages to return to England.

The story of this most curious romance may be read in the novel *Peter Wilkins* (1751) by Robert Paltock.

The Zaratan

There is a story that is told in all lands and throughout all history—the story of sailors who go ashore on an unknown island that later sinks and drowns them, for the island is alive. This imaginary beast-island figures in the first voyage of Sindbad and in the sixth canto of *Orlando Furioso* (*Ch'ella sia una isoletta ci credemo;* "We all are cheated by the floating pile, / And idly take the monster for an isle"); in the Irish legend of St. Brendan and in the Greek bestiary of Alexandria; in the Swedish curate Olaf Magnus' *History of the Northern Nations* (Rome, 1555) and in that passage in *Paradise Lost*, Book I, in which the prostrate Satan is compared to a great whale "hap'ly slumbering on the Norway foam."

Paradoxically, one of the first versions of the legend recounts it only to refute it. Al-Yahiz, a ninth-century Muslim zoologist, includes it in his *Book of the Animals.* Miguel Asín Palacios translated the passage into Spanish, and we render it to the reader here in English:

> As for the Zaratan, I have never seen anyone who can swear that he has seen it with his own eyes.
>
> Some sailors claim sometimes to have approached certain ocean isles whereupon woods and valleys and crevices are to be found, and to have lighted fires; and when the fire hath reached the back of the Zaratan, it hath begun to glide [through the water] with them [atop it] and with all the plants thereupon, until at last only he who manageth to flee may save himself. This tale surpasses all the most fabulous and brazen stories.

Let us look for a moment now at a thirteenth-century text. It was written by the Muslim cosmographer Al-Qazwini and is taken from his work titled *The Wonders of Creation:*

> As for the sea-turtle, it is of such enormous size that the people of the ship take it for an island. One of the merchants told the following story:
>
> "We discovered in the sea an island that rose out of the water, with green plants, and we went ashore and in the ground we dug pits to cook in, and the island moved, and the sailors cried: 'Come back! for it is a tortoise, and the heat of the fire has awakened it, and we may all be lost!'"

In *The Voyage of St. Brendan,* the story is told again:

> When they approached the other island, the boat began to ground before they could reach its landing-place. Saint Brendan ordered the brothers to disembark from the boat into the sea, which they did. . . . The island was stony and without grass. There were a few pieces of driftwood on it, but no sand on its shore. . . . While Saint Brendan was himself singing his Mass in the boat, the brothers began to carry the raw meat out of the boat to preserve it with salt, and also the flesh which they had brought from the other island. When they had done this they put a pot over a fire. When, however, they were plying the fire with wood and the pot began to boil, the island began to be in motion like a wave. The brothers rushed to the boat, crying out for protection to the holy father. He drew each one of them into the boat by his hand. Having left everything they had had on the island behind, they began to sail. Then the island moved out to sea. The lighted fire could be

seen over two miles away. Saint Brendan told the brother what it really was, saying:

"Brothers, are you surprised at what this island has done?"

They said:

"We are very surprised and indeed terror-stricken."

He said to them:

"My sons, do not be afraid. . . . Where we were was not an island, but a fish—the foremost of all that swim in the ocean. He is always trying to bring his tail to meet his head, but he cannot because of his length. His name is Jasconius."*

In the Anglo-Saxon bestiary called the *Exeter Book,* this dangerous island is a whale, "cunninge in evil," which deceives men deliberately. Seeking rest from the travails of the sea, sailors make camp upon its back; suddenly this Ocean Guest submerges and the sailors are all drowned. In the Greek bestiary, the Whale is the harlot of Proverbs 5:5 ("Her feet go down to death; her steps take hold on hell"); in the Anglo-Saxon bestiary, it is the devil, Evil. It retains this symbolic value in *Moby-Dick,* which was written a thousand years later.

*Cf. *Ouroboros,* p. 147

Translator's Note

Perhaps the best known of all of Jorge Luis Borges' stories, "Tlön, Uqbar, Orbis Tertius," turns on the discovery of an encyclopedia—a pirated and retitled edition of the 1902 *Encyclopædia Britannica* which, to the befuddlement and then growing astonishment of the narrator, contains an entry for an imaginary country, the land of Uqbar, which is very much like, yet very much unlike, countries that we are all familiar with. In that astounding and possibly apocryphal entry in a very real and precisely numbered Volume XLVI, the narrator, "Borges," reads of a host of things that are almost, but not quite, believable, among them transparent tigers.

That intriguing note, rung as early as 1940, attains the complexity of a Bach fugue in this volume, *The Book of Imaginary Beings*, for this book is itself an encyclopedia (or if it is not quite so complete as an encyclopedia, it at least has the alphabetical organization of one); it details 116 instances of creatures as marvelous and strange as transparent tigers; and, of course, the creatures it details are imaginary in exactly the way those famous transparent tigers are: they are stitched together, like Dr. Frankenstein's creation, out of the parts of real creatures, but the whole is a whole that is impossible, "fantastic," never seen in nature. In addition, this fantastic encyclopedia, like that earlier alphabetized universe, has "penetrated" our own: the imaginary beings it chronicles are creatures we have lived with and think of as "normal" aspects of our world—if not our real world, then the inner world of our fantasies and dreams and fears. And so, as in so many of Borges' fictions, we are made to look at things and ourselves anew, and to wonder at the richness of his and our imaginations.

This is a book that is sometimes as amazing as the creatures it presents, then, yet that one might almost think was inevitable, given Borges' lifelong fascination with tigers, books—or, more specifically, miscellanies; more specifically yet, encyclopedias—, erudite and abstruse researches, and put-ons. The volume, even more than the individual pieces in it, is perhaps the clearest and most concentrated example of what I see as the very essence of Borges' writing: its simultaneous seriousness and playfulness. What a wonderful philosophical and aesthetic, if somewhat private, joke—producing a book of fiction (or fictions) that is organized alphabetically, like a reference work! But analyzing the complexity of that idea, beginning with the definition of "fiction" for the work of Jorge Luis Borges, would be a labor of decades, so I will not even begin to attempt it here—except to note that this work, like Borges' very earliest fictions, is both highly original and a pastiche of sources, styles, literary genres, cultures . . . ; that like all his work, it is filled with philosophical notions treated imaginatively, creatively, always under the banner of *Als Ob*; that it contains, as Borges himself notes in the Foreword, both horror (alienation) and fun, or, like a John Barth funhouse, fun *because* horror; that it is an interrogation as much as an exemplification of the work of the human imagination; that while it is often utterly convincing as truth, it is clearly bracketed with the quotation marks of fiction; that in confronting us with the very definition of what a work of fiction is, it is a metafiction before its time. Like so many of Borges' other works, it takes an existing and "secondary" form of literature—science fiction or biography or the mystery story; here, specifically, the medieval bestiary—and makes it central to the concerns of art. It is a work that is, like the creatures it contains, sui generis yet absolutely recognizable, and its very existence is cause for the kind of exhilaration that a reader always feels in the presence of a work that is both brilliant and absolutely right.

The publishing history of this work is interesting in itself. In 1957, Borges first published a book entitled *Manual de Zoología Fantástica, A Manual of Fantastic Zoology*, which he had written (or compiled) in collaboration with Margarita Guerrero. It was published by the prestigious Fonda de Cultura Económica in Mexico City and Buenos Aires and contained a preface and eighty-two entries, arranged basically in alphabetical order, though there were two pieces, "Antelopes with Six Legs" (translated here literally, for effect) and "Baldanders," appended to the very *end* of the book, totally out of order; they follow the "Zaratan." This same arrangement was reissued in 1966 and 1971 by the original publisher.

In 1967, a new version of the book was published in Buenos Aires by the publishing company Kier; its title was now *El libro de los seres imaginarios,* or *The Book of Imaginary Beings.* This volume was brought out in a larger format than the first (approximately eight inches wide by nine inches tall) and for many of the beasts there were illustrations by Silvio Baldessari. Margarita Guerrero's co-authorship was still acknowledged. To the eighty-two pieces of the original volume were added thirty-four additional ones, bringing the total to 116; there was a new preface, and the older one was dropped. In this edition, the order of the pieces was extensively rearranged; those original to the *Manual* were arranged in only very approximate alphabetical order, and the new ones were interspersed without any rhyme or reason that I can make out. (For example, toward the end of the book came the Brownies, followed by the Valkyries and then the Norns.) Sometimes the new pieces were *almost* alphabetically inserted, other times not even that close.

In 1969, an English-language version (not to call it, in strict terms, a *translation* of either prior Spanish-language collection) was published by E. P. Dutton in New York, followed in 1970 by the British Jonathan Cape edition using the same text; its title was *The Book of Imaginary Beings*. This edition, while still more or less acknowledging Margarita Guerrero's co-authorship of the Spanish original, spelled (travestied) her name as "Margaritta Guerro," at least in the Avon paperback that followed, and the new preface somewhat confusingly employed a "we" dually initialed "J.L.B." and *not* "M.G." but rather "N.T.diG." Further information on the clearly complex authorship of this English version was provided by a title page stating that the book had been "Revised, Enlarged and Translated by Norman Thomas di Giovanni in collaboration with the Author" (singular). The "enlargement" consisted of four new entries: "The Carbuncle," "An Experimental Account of What Was Known, Seen, and Met by Mrs. Jane Lead in London in 1694," "Fauna of Chile," and *"Laudatores Temporis Acti."* I do not know where these pieces came from; hopefully one of the new biographies now being readied for publication will throw some light on this point. Otherwise it is impossible to say whether Borges himself, independent of collaboration, had any of these pieces in his pocket prior to this edition, though he certainly may have had: the foreword to the 1967 edition makes the following request: "We [JLB and Margarita Guerrero] invite [this book's] eventual readers in Colombia or Paraguay to send us the names, reliable descriptions, and most conspicuous habits of their own local monsters." Thus, it would not be surprising, I think, though this is the purest sort of speculation, had "Fauna of Chile" been in Borges' possession for some time, waiting for a new edition. Two of the other three added pieces are from English sources, and may (or, of course, may not) have been suggested by Mr. Di Giovanni. The entries in this edition are in strict alphabetical order.

When the text of this English edition is compared to that of the 1967 Spanish-language edition that preceded it, one sees that the statement that the Dutton edition was "revised" from the Spanish is well founded. Just one example of many possible: the piece on the Pygmies in the prior edition was expanded by two phrases (in a space of two brief paragraphs) in the English translation. Other times, paragraphs were added or moved about.

In 1978, Emecé in Buenos Aires published, under Emecé copyright, a new (paperback) edition of something very much like the 1967 Kier version of the book: It was still titled as in 1967, the contents were the same, but several "pairs" of pieces were inverted. (I put quotation marks around the word "pairs" because the beings whose entries were inverted are not related subjects or species, or associated by any principle that I can fathom; my assumption is that because copyright law is written in the peculiar way it sometimes is, the *order* of the entries, the fictions, had to be changed if a new copyright was to be secured.) In this new edition there was no attempt to "repair" the loss of alphabetical-orderliness inflicted on the book (if that was the case) by Kier. This volume had no illustrations.

Interestingly, while a note in this new edition acknowledged the publication in English, in 1969/1970, of the Dutton/Jonathan Cape edition of *The Book of Imaginary Beings* (no translator's name given), this new edition omitted the four pieces added there. This is unusual in the publishing history of this book, as no other volume ever returned to an earlier, lesser number of beings or omitted whole sentences and paragraphs. Once again: The Emecé edition, though later than the 1969 English edition, and acknowledging it (and therefore, one would ordinarily assume, acknowledging Borges' intentions for the book), mysteriously neither "revises" any of its text along the lines indicated by the English nor retains the additions included there.

In 1981, Burguera, in Barcelona, republished the text of the 1967/1978 *Libro de los seres imaginarios*, though in this case strictly observing alphabetical order among the entries. The title page of this edition dropped the name of Margarita Guerrero, though the preface, identical to the 1967 foreword, and dated that year, bore her initials along with Borges'. The copyright for this edition was acknowledged to belong to Emecé, not Burguera, and it was dated 1978.

The reader can see, then, that certain decisions had to be made as to the text to be used for this translation. It has seemed clear to me that the pieces in the volume were sometimes rearranged simply so that a new copyright could be obtained on the raw materials of the collection; thus, I have opted to put the pieces in alphabetical order, as the first and last editions made in Borges' life had them. Likewise, attempting to discern Borges' intentions as apart from those of collaborators and companies who wished to secure new copyrights, I have decided that had Borges wished to include the additions and revisions made to the English version of the book, those additions and revisions would have been incorporated into the subsequent Spanish-language edition, which was published by Borges' "official" publishing house of the time, Emecé, in Buenos Aires, while he was still very much alive. But they were not. The volume as it appears here, then, collects the eighty-four original pieces of the *Manual de Zoología Fantástica* and the thirty-two pieces subsequently added to *Spanish-language* editions, plus the two "original" forewords. The reader may disagree with this decision, may wish that the four pieces added in the English volume had been included here and that this volume also contained the Borges–di Giovanni foreword to that collection; but the selection reflects what I believe a reasonable person might infer from currently available bibliographical evidence to be Borges' personal aesthetic intentions for the book, independent of any external considerations.

Another problem, this time dealing with translation, per se, was presented by Borges' method of composition for these pieces. The book, as I noted earlier, is a sort of "pastiche," weaving together material from an almost literally countless number of authors. It is clear that for much of the material in the original Spanish—sometimes entire "entries"—Borges was translating directly from a source, acknowledged in many cases, unacknowledged in many others, or was using a Spanish translation of a "classic." Quite often, he seems to have been translating (or rewriting) into Spanish from an English translation from, for example, the Greek. Thus, rather than translate Borges' translations, themselves perhaps done from translations, I have gone to the original (where I could find it) or the standard, canonical English version of a classic, following Borges' "editing" where he changed details in the text. I should note that there are times when Borges says he is "summarizing" a source yet in fact is very closely following it; there, I have, as before, used the source as much as possible. If he was not so clearly "cribbing" from the original, but truly summarizing or paraphrasing it, then I simply translate his Spanish.

Because I have chosen this method of "translating" Borges for this volume, I have thought it necessary—not least because of copyright considerations—to document the source of material I have (or Borges, in a roundabout way, has) quoted from. Thus, the notes that follow this text can be thought of as acknowledgment of the clear textual borrowings in this volume. Where Borges bows to the author but does not directly quote him or her, no note will appear; *mutatis mutandis,* where no note is given for a phrase or other piece of text that is enclosed within quotation marks, I am translating from Borges' Spanish, which was itself in quotation marks, but I have not been able to track down Borges' source. The nature of Borges' erudition, creativity, and sense of fun is such that it has been simply impossible to ferret out all the originals, where originals in fact ever existed (some of his "quotations" are almost certainly apocryphal, put-ons). I did attempt to track everything down, and the absence of notes where they might be expected is a source of some chagrin to me, not to mention awe at Borges' wide reading.

My only fear in choosing this strategy for documenting the sources that Borges used is that the notes may make the book seem stodgier, more academic, less fun than it was clearly always meant to be. I hope that readers of this volume, dipping into it here and there as Borges hoped they would, will not lose (or be stripped of) their sense of playfulness by feeling that they have to go look up the page numbers for Pliny—think of it as just another of Borges' ways of blurring lines between the serious and the playful.

Where footnotes appear in the text, they are (with the exceptions acknowledged within the notes themselves) Borges', and appeared in the original Spanish.

—Andrew Hurley
San Juan, Puerto Rico
July 1999
June 2004

Notes

p. 5 *Tundale's vision of the monster Acheron:* It seems likely that Borges took this description from the Middle English version of the monster in the Cotton ms., ll. 487–592 (*The Vision of Tundale*, ed. from B.L. MS Cotton Caligula A II by Rodney Mearns, Heidelberg: Carl Winter, Universitätsverlag [Middle English Texts series, No. 18], 1985, pp. 97–100). Here are the pertinent lines of that description, in the Middle English (with modern alphabet for greater comprehensibility):

> [492] But they sawe then a hydwys sygth,
> They sawe a beste was more to knawe
> Then all the mountaynes that they before sawe,
>
> And hys yen semede more
> And bradder then the halses wore.
> In at hys mowthe that was so wyde
> Nyne thowsand armed men mygth in ryde.
> Betwyx hys tuskus that wer so longe
> Two grete gyantes sawe he honge;
> The hedde of that on henge all downe
> And that other hede to hys crowne.
> In myddes hys mowgth on ylke a syde
> Tho pylers were sette to holde hyt vppe wyde.
>
> Al thre grete gates that open stode
> The flames of fyr out at hem gode,
> And therof come as foul a stynke
> And sayde to the angell brygth:
> "What menes that hydwys sygth?"
> As any erthely mon may thynke.
> He herde therin a delfull dyn
> Of mony thowsand sowles wythin.
> Gowlynge & gretynge he herde amonge,
> And "Wellaway!" was euer her songe.
> Lowde he herde hem crye & gelle,
> Her sorow mygth no tonge telle.

Before the bestes mowthe they sene
Mony a thowsand deuelles full kene
That hyede hem wyth mygth & mayne
Tho wrecched sowlus to bete & payne,
Wyth brennande bables on hem they donge
And wythin hem frowe to paynes stronge.

When Tundale thys beeste hadde sene,
And tho wykkede gostes that wer so kene,
And hadde herde that hydwys cry,
Tundale spakke full delfully

And sayde to the angell Grygth:
"What means that hydwys sygth?"

The angell answered hym anon:
"Thys beeste ys called Acheron,
And herforth behoueth vs to wende
Gyf we sholde go to our wayes ende; . . ."
[533] This hydwys beste, as I the kenne,
Is sette to swolewe coueytows menne,
In prophecye ys wryten thus:
"A beeste shall swolewe the coueytows."

[554] The angell vanyshched & he stode styll,
No wonther gyf he hadde grete drede!
The fowle gostes come to hym good spede;
They toke hym tho & donge hym faste,
Wythinne the beste they gon hym caste.
A whyle wythinne behoueth hym to dwelle,
Ther was he beten wyth fendes felle,
Wyth kene howndys that on hym gnewe,
And dragones that hym all todrewe,
Wyth edderes & snakes & other vermyne
He was gnawen in ylke a lyme.
Now was he hote wyth fyr brennande,
And now yn yse colde fresande.
The teres of hys yen twoo
Brennede as fyr, so was he woo.
Stronge stynke he felde of brymston,
he was yn paynes mony on.

P. 7 *"walks upright like a walking-stick"*: This is the translation of the quotation given by Borges. In the translation by Robert Graves (Lucan, *The Pharsalia*, trans. Robert Graves, Harmondsworth, Middlesex: Penguin Books, 1956), which I have otherwise attempted to use throughout this volume, the original is translated "plows a furrow as it goes," and that phrasing is pretty consistent throughout the various English versions of the *Pharsalia* and of the other works that mention this beast—most famously, perhaps, Pliny. I give Borges', however, for the grotesqueness; Graves's is fairly tame in that regard, since this "mark" or "characteristic" is one that all snakes no doubt share.

P. 7 *"as though one mouth were too little for the discharge of all its venom"*: The Natural History of Pliny, with copious notes and illustrations, in six volumes, John Bostock and H. T. Riley, London: Henry G. Bohn, 1855, Vol. II, p. 285. All subsequent references to Pliny or the *Natural History* will be to this edition, noted as "Vol: page." Generally, JLB gives the "Book" and "Chapter" numbers in the text himself, for those readers who have other editions.

P. 7 *"there is no inferiour or former part in this animall"*: Sir Thomas Browne, *Pseudodoxia Epidemica* (two volumes), ed. Robin Robbins, Oxford: Oxford University Press, 1981, Vol. I, p. 217. All subsequent references to Browne's *Pseudodoxia* will be to this edition, given as "Vol.: page."

P. 10 *"An Animal Dreamed by Kafka"*: Franz Kafka, "Fragments," in *Dearest Father: Stories and Other Writings*, trans. Ernst Kaiser and Eithne Wilkins, New York: Schocken, 1954, pp. 297–98.

P. 11 *"An Animal Dreamed by C. S. Lewis"*: C. S. Lewis, *Perelandra*, London: John Lane The Bodley Head, 1943, p. 219.

P. 13 *"The Animal Dreamed by Poe"*: Edgar Allan Poe, *The Narrative of Arthur Gordon Pym of Nantucket*, New York: Hill and Wang, 1960 (first published 1837), pp. 145, 150.

P. 20 *"uniform circular motion on the same spot"*: Plato, *Timæus*, trans. with an introduction by H. D. P. Lee, Baltimore: Penguin Books, 1965, ¶ 33.

P. 23 the Three-Legged Ass of the Bundahish: adapted, according to JLB's usage, from *The Bundahishn ("Creation")*, or *Knowledge from the Zand*, trans. E. W. West, in *Sacred Books of the East*, London/NY: Oxford University Press, 1897, Vol. 5, Chap. 19, n.p. (www.aresta.org/pahlaril/bund18.html).

P. 25 *"The earth was, it is said . . ."*: Edward William Lane, *Arabian Society in the Middle Ages: Studies from* The Thousand and One Nights, ed. Stanley Lane-Poole, introd. by C. E. Bosworth, New Jersey: Humanities Press, 1987, pp. 106–107 (repr. of the 1883 edition, with a new introd). Subsequent references to Lane's *Arabian Society* will be to this edition, by page.

P. 26 *Burton's description of the Bahamut:* Sir Richard Francis Burton, *The Book of the Thousand Nights and a Night: A Plain and Literal Translation of the Arabian Nights Entertainments,* in six volumes, New York: G. Macy Companies, 1962 (a reprint of the Ltd. Editions Club 1934 reprint of the 1885 original edition), Night 496 (vol. 2, pp. 1927–28). All subsequent references to Burton's *Nights* will, unless otherwise noted, refer to this edition.

P. 30 *"with a white spot on the head, strongly resembling a sort of a diadem":* Pliny, II: 282.

P. 30 *"Medusa is said to have lived . . .":* Lucan, *Pharsalia: Dramatic Episodes of the Civil Wars,* trans. Robert Graves, Harmondsworth, Middlesex, England: Penguin Books, 1956, pp. 213–15. Subsequent references to the *Pharsalia* will be to this text.

P. 31 The *"effluvium of the weasel is fatal to it":* Pliny, II: 282.

P. 33 *Note: the royal "we":* Here, Borges supplies a note based on Spanish grammar; I have simply inserted its English-language equivalent.

P. 38 *Sir Thomas Browne's description of the Borametz:* Browne, *Pseudodoxia Epidemica,* I: 289. Other sources spell this creature's name as "Barometz" or "Baromez," and give its Latin name as not *Polypodium* but rather *Lycopodium,* although today most scientific botanists take it to have been a rhizome of the arborescent fern *Cibotium borametz,* native to China. The first mention of this creature in English seems to be in Sir John Mandeville's *Travels,* Chapter 29, paragraph 3, where one finds the following description of a meal he partook of in Tartary: "And there groweth a manner of fruit, as though it were gourds. And when they be ripe, men cut them a-two, and men find within a little beast, in flesh, in bone, and blood, as though it were a little lamb without wool. And men eat both the fruit and the beast. And that is a great marvel" (David Price, editor, New York: Macmillan & Co., 1900). It was this description that gave the creature the common name it was subsequently known by, the "vegetable lamb of Tartary."

P. 38 *forest of suicides from whose "broken splints come words and blood at once":* Dante, *The Divine Comedy: 1: Hell,* trans. Dorothy L. Sayers, New York: Penguin Books (Classic), 1949, p. 130. (Canto XIII: Circle VII, Ring ii, The Wood of the Suicides.) Subsequent references to Dante's *Inferno* will be to this text.

p. 41 *Miguel Asín Palacios:* A distinguished Spanish Arabist, perhaps the most distinguished of the twentieth century, and one of the first modern commentators to discuss openly and "scientifically" the influence of Islam on Spanish literature and life, which had been a virtually forbidden topic theretofore. Asín is as famous in the hispanophone academy as his anglophone counterparts F. R. Leavis and William Empson.

p. 43 *"An animal of moderate size":* Pliny, II: 281–82.

p. 43 *Temptation of St. Anthony on the Catoblepas:* Gustave Flaubert, *The Temptation of St. Anthony,* trans. Lafcadio Hearn, New York: Grosset & Dunlap, n.d., p. 159. Subsequent references to the *Temptation* will be to this edition, by page.

p. 45 *Prescott on Centaurs:* William H. Prescott, *History of the Conquest of Mexico and History of the Conquest of Peru,* New York: Random House (Modern Library), n.d., p. 859.

p. 46 *Plutarch on a "Centaur":* Plutarch, *Moralia,* Vol. II, "The Dinner of the Seven Wise Men," with an English trans. by Frank Cole Babbitt, New York: G. P. Putnam's Sons (Loeb), 1928, pp. 365–67.

p. 47 *"Centaurs never existed, . . .":* Lucretius, *De rerum natura,* with an English translation by W. H. D. Rouse, rev., with new text, introduction, notes, and index by Martin Ferguson Smith, 2nd ed. Cambridge, MA: Harvard University Press, 1982, V: 878–91.

p. 49 *Butler's description of Cerberus:* Samuel Butler, *Hudibras: in Three Parts, Written in the Time of the Late Wars: Corrected and Amended, with Large Annotations, and a Preface,* by Zachary Grey, LL.D. (2 vols.), Cambridge: J. Bentham, MDCCXLIV, Vol. II, p. 282 (Pt. III, Canto II, ll. 661ff):

> For as the *Pope,* that keeps the Gate
> Of Heaven, wears three Crowns of State;
> So he that keeps the Gate of Hell,
> Proud *Cerberus,* wears three Heads as well:
> And, if the World has any Troth,
> Some have been canoniz'd in both.

p. 49 *"his eyeballs glare . . .":* Dante, trans. Sayers, Canto VI, ll. 13ff., p. 104.

p. 49 *"This Dog with three Heads . . .":* Samuel Butler, *Hudibras, op. cit.* Vol. I, p. 15, note to l. 103 (i.e., one of Grey's annotations to Butler's poem).

p. 51 *"her forepart [was] lionish, . . .":* Homer, *The Iliad,* trans. Robert Fitzgerald, Garden City, NY: Doubleday Anchor, 1975, VI: ll. 156–58,

p. 147. Hesiod (see note below) says that she "snorted raging fire" (*Theogony*, l. 319).

P. 51 *"Her heads were three . . .":* Hesiod, *op.cit.*, ll. 322–25.

P. 51 *"breathing dangerous flames":* Virgil, *The Æneid*, trans. Robert Fitzgerald, New York: Random House (Vintage), 1984, VI: l. 394 (289), p. 169.

P. 54 *"a wild beast of extraordinary swiftness, . . .":* Pliny, II: 279. T. H. White informs us that the "Crocuta," the offspring of the "Yena" and a Lioness, seems to have been the hyæna, and that its name has appeared variously as Leucrota, Crocuta, Corocotta, Ceucrocuta, etc., but that the "Leucrocuta," as described by Pliny and others, may have been the Mantichora, "which in the Persian tongue signifieth a devourer of men." (T. H. White, *The Book of Beasts: Being a Translation from a Latin Bestiary of the Twelfth Century*, New York: Dover, 1984 (1954), pp. 32n., 48.)

P. 55 *"A Crossbreed":* Franz Kafka, *Description of a Struggle and The Great Wall of China*, "A Crossbreed," trans. Willa and Edwin Muir, London: Secker & Warburg, publ. 1960, © 1933 (Schocken Books, © 1958), original German © 1936, 1937 by Heinr, Mercy Sohn, Prague (Schocken, © 1946). (This bibliographical information is taken verbatim from the copyright page of the book from which this long quotation is taken; I have simply reproduced the apparent confusion I found there.)

P. 60 *"Liberation Through Hearing . . .":* The Tibetan Book of the Dead: or, The After-Death Experiences on the Bardo Plane, according to Lama Kazi Dawa-Samdup's English Rendering,* compiled and edited by W. Y. Evans-Wentz, London/New York: Oxford University Press, 1969, p. xvi.

P. 64 *Willoughby-Meade on the types of Dragons:* Gerald Willoughby-Meade, *Chinese Ghouls and Goblins*, London: Constable & Co., 1928, p. 145.

P. 68 *on the crushed Dragon:* "Cinnabaris," Pliny tells us (VI, 38), was "the name given to the thick matter which issues from the dragon when crushed beneath the weight of the dying elephant. . . . [It] is the only colour that in painting gives a proper representation of blood." This "matter" was not to be confused, Pliny warns us, with "miltos," or red ochre, peroxide of iron "mixed with argillaceous earth."

P. 68 *Pliny on the medicinal uses of the Dragon:* Pliny, V: 395.

P. 77 *Fastitocalon in Anglo-Saxon bestiary: Codex Exoniensis: A Collection of Anglo-Saxon Poetry, from a manuscript in the Library of the Dean and Chapter of Exeter*, with an English translation, notes, and indexes, by Benjamin Thorpe, F.S.A., London: Society of Antiquaries of London, 1842, pp. 360–65.

p. 83 *Fauna of the United States:* Wry descriptions of these creatures, in more or less the abbreviated form that JLB seems to have been quoting, were published in Charles Edward Brown, *Paul Bunyan Natural History: Describing the Wild Animals, Birds, Reptiles and Fish of the Big Woods about Paul Bunyan's Old Time Logging Camps* . . . [etc.], Madison, Wisconsin: C. E. Brown [self-published?], 1935, a pamphletlike publication totaling eight pages (though there is an earlier Brown publication, in 1922, that summarily presents some, but not all, of these animals). They also appear in various dictionaries and collections of folklore; it is difficult to say precisely which source JLB might have been "quoting," but the remarkable coincidence of much of the wording leads the translator to believe it must have been this pamphlet.

p. 90 *In the Talmud: Hebrew-English Edition of the Babylonian Talmud: Sanhedrin,* trans. H. Freedman, ed. Rabbi Dr. I. Epstein, London: Sorcino Press, 1969.

p. 91 *the footnote on Schopenhauer:* Here, Borges' footnote is translated verbatim from the Spanish, though the text in the most recent English translation of Schopenhauer is very different; it is hard to tell whether Borges has interpolated certain information ("the English visionary Jane Lead[e]") into Schopenhauer or whether that information appeared in the edition from which he was quoting, whatever that edition might have been. (Two other English translations preceded the current one, and Schopenhauer himself existed in several editions in German; the translator is not able to assess the status of the Spanish translations, if any.) The modern translation reads as follows: "In his *Zauberbibliothek* (Vol. I, p. 325) Horst quotes the following passage from the *Offenbarung der Offenbarungen.* [i.e., Revelation of Revelations, but with a *German* title!] But [this passage] is more a *resumé* than a literal quotation, and is taken mainly from page 119, §§ 87 and 88: 'Magic power enables its possessor to rule and renew creation, viz., the plant, animal, and mineral kingdoms, so that if *many* cooperated in *one* magic power, nature could be creatively turned into a paradise.'" (Arthur Schopenhauer, *On the Will in Nature: A Discussion of the Corroborations from the Empirical Sciences that the Author's Philosophy has Received Since Its First Appearance,* trans. E. F. J. Payne, ed. with an Introduction by David E. Cartwright, New York/Oxford: Berg (St. Martin's Press), 1992, p. 125.)

Before we consider the differences between this text and the footnote that Borges gives, let us first consider "the English visionary Jane Lead[e]" (1624–1704). She was a theosophist and disciple of Dr. John Pordage, who introduced her to the writings of Jacob Boehme (1575–1624), an important German mystic. Her book is titled in English *Revelation of Revelations: Particularly as an Essay towards the Unsealing, Opening and Discovering, the Seven Seals, the Seven Thunders, and the New Jerusalem State*, and the bibliographical information reads as follows: "Publ. by J.L. the author of The Heavenly Cloud [etc.], London, Printed and Sold by A. Sowle [!] at the Crooked-Billet in Holloway Lane in Shoreditch . . . 1683." Thus, one suspects that Payne, Schopenhauer's translator above, has not gone to the original of Leade's work, but rather has used Schopenhauer's (or Horst's) footnote, which gave Leade's title in German. The translator seems not even to have identified the original author.

Then there is the issue of the differences between Borges' quotation and this one. Not only does this edition (Payne? Cartwright?) give the title of Leade's work in German, rather than in English; differences between the "quotation" given here and anything in Leade, as well as differences between two further "quotations" in the Schopenhauer translation and the actual wording of Leade's text, not to mention a discrepancy in page numbering between this citation and the real page numbers of Leade's original work, lead one to assert that Schopenhauer's translator translated from Schopenhauer's (or someone else's) German translation of Leade and that the German translation must garble Leade considerably. Horst's summary certainly does so. It is true that Horst's "quotation" is only a summary; but one must in conscience call it a *bad* summary, for one can find almost no traces of the ideas Horst attributes to Leade in Leade herself, for one might look in vain on pp. 58–60 (the apposite location, according to the page and paragraph numbers as quoted by Payne) for the words that Horst is said to summarize. (That almost absolute discrepancy is the reason I am not quoting Leade: I wouldn't know what to quote.) One can only speculate that Leade, who did exist in at least one German edition, had been somewhat freely translated and that Horst somewhat freely summarized her from that. Nonetheless, there is no doubt that Horst's version supported Schopenhauer and what Schopenhauer wanted to find (i.e., other authorities asserting the power of the Will), and that Schopenhauer in turn supported what JLB needed.

P. 91 *"The original story harks back . . .":* Gustav Meyrink, *The Golem*, trans. Madge Pemberton, Boston: Houghton Mifflin, 1928, p. 41.

P. 93 *Mandeville on the Gryphon: The Travels of Sir John Mandeville (The version of the Cotton Manuscript in modern spelling)*, London: Macmillan and Co., 1915, p. 177. The Bodleian Text, as transcribed by Malcolm Letts, *Mandeville's Travels*, in two vols., London: Hakluyt Society, 1953, Vol. II., pp. 463–64, reads as follows:

And in that londe growen trees that bereth wolle, but it is gret and royde [stout]. And folke of that cuntre maketh hem clothis theroff forto were. And ther is also a manere of beestis that men calle iro-tamus. And they ben as wel in watir as in the londe, and they haue the half shappe of a man and the tother half of an hors. And thes beestis wole eten men rather thenne any othir thing ellis. And ther arn also grefouns, that haue the fourme of eglis bifore, and the fourme of a lioun byhynde. And he is more strengere thenne vij. liouns, ffor a grefoun wole bere to his nest bothe hors and man, or twoo oxen yoked in a plowy. And the clees of his feete arn as mochel as an oxe horn, and men of that cuntre maken of hem cuppis forto drynke of, and of his ffetheris they make bowes to shoote with.

P. 94 *Dante on the Gryphon:* Dante, *The Divine Comedy: 2: Purga-tory,* trans. Dorothy L. Sayers, New York: Penguin Books (Classic), 1955, Canto XXIX, ll. 107–14, p. 301. Subsequent references to *The Divine Comedy* will be to this edition.

P. 98 *Ezekiel's vision:* In King James, Ezekiel 1:10, 12, 18.

P. 101 *"Cain with his thorn-bush":* Dante, *Hell,* trans. Sayers, p. 198.

P. 102 *"Buddha," we are told . . . :* G. Willoughby-Meade, *Chinese Ghosts and Goblins,* London: Constable & Co. Ltd., 1928, p. 168.

P. 103 *winged deities "of lovely hair":* Hesiod: *The Works and Days, Theogony, The Shield of Herakles,* trans. Richmond Lattimore, Ann Ar-bor: University of Michigan Press, 1959, p. 139. Subsequent references to Hesiod's *Theogony* will be to this edition, cited by page.

P. 103 *Ariosto turns the king of Thrace . . . :* While Borges did not in-clude Ariosto's description of the Harpies (*The Orlando Furioso of Ludo-vico Ariosto,* trans. William Stewart Rose, London: G. Bell & Sons, Ltd. [New York: Macmillan], 1913), it must be acknowledged to be equally as horrible as Virgil's, perhaps more so:

> All bear a female face of pallid dye,
>   And seven in number are the horrid band;
>   Emaciated with hunger, lean, and dry;
>   Fouler than death; the pinions they expand
>   Ragged, and huge, and shapeless to the eye;
>   The talon crook'd; rapacious is the hand;
>   Fetid and large the paunch; in many a fold,
>   Like snake's, their long and knotted tails are rolled.

The fowls are heard in air; then swoops amain
  The covey well nigh in that instant, rends
  The food, o'erturns the vessels, and a rain
  Of noisome ordure on the board descends.
  To stop their nostrils king and duke are fain;
  Such an insufferable stench offends.

P. 103 *raptor:* William Morris calls them "snatchers."

P. 104 *Ariosto's precise description of the Hippogriff:* Ariosto, *Orlando Furioso, op. cit.,* Canto IV: xviii, p. 53. These are the lines in question:

No empty fiction wrought by magic lore,
  But natural was the steed the wizard pressed:
  For him a filly to a griffin bore;
  Hight hippogryph. In wings and beak and crest,
  Formed like his sire, as in the feet before;
  But like the mare, his dam, in all the rest.
  Such on Riphaean hills, though rarely found,
  Are bred, beyond the frozen ocean's bound.

P. 104 *second reference to Ariosto's Hippogriff: Ibid.,* II: xxxvii, p. 25.

P. 105 *further lines on the Hippogriff: Ibid.,* IV: iv, p. 50.

P. 107 *the Humbaba:* Yet in other translations, these characteristics are not so clear, and in fact Humbaba seems to be something of a shapeshifter, like a Babylonian Proteus; this is true not just at the level of "imaginary being," but also at the level of text, for it is hard to see how translators can translate the "same" text in so many ways. Let us look at just two examples. This first description is from *The Epic of Gilgamesh, An English Version* by N. K. Sandars, Baltimore: Penguin (Classics), 1960:

Gilgamesh seized the axe in his hand; he felled the cedar. "Who is this that has violated my woods and cut down my cedar?" . . .

"By the life of Ninsun my mother who gave me birth, and by the life of my father divine Lugulbanda, until we have fought this man, if man he is, this god, if god he is, the way that I took to the Country of the Living will not turn back to the city."

Then Enkidu, the faithful companion, pleaded, answering him, "O my lord, you do not know this monster and that is the reason you are not afraid. I who know him, I am terrified. His teeth are dragon's fangs, his countenance is like a lion, his charge is the rushing of the flood, with his look he crushes alike the trees of the forest and reeds in the swamp."

Another, even later, translation (*Gilgamesh: A New Rendering in English Verse*, David Ferry, New York: Farrar, Straus and Giroux, 1992) gives the same passage as follows:

> This was the place Huwawa was; Huwawa's
> Breath is death. Beautiful is the Forest;
>
> green upon green the cedars; fragrant the air
> with the fragrance of cedar trees; the box that grew
>
> along the silent walks of the guardian demon,
> shadowed and still, utterly still, was fragrant.
>
> Then Gilgamesh was afraid, and Enkidu
> was afraid, and they entered into the Forest, afraid,
>
> the two of them together, and felled some cedars.
> The guardian of the Cedar Forest roared. . . .
>
> Always the face of Huwawa was somewhere there.
> There was the noise of swords, daggers, and axes,
>
> confusions of noises in the Cedar Forest.
> Then Gilgamesh saw the face of Huwawa the demon
>
> And fled from the face, hiding himself away. . . .
> Then Gilgamesh said: "The face of Huwawa keeps changing!"

Indeed a more terrifying monster than this is hard to imagine; its very description seems to be beyond the powers of man, and translator.

p. 110 *Typhon:* Typhon, Robert Graves tells us, was "the largest monster ever born. From the thighs downward he was nothing but coiled serpents, and his arms which, when he spread them out, reached a hundred leagues in either direction, had countless serpents' heads instead of hands. His brutish ass-head touched the stars, his vast wings darkened the sun, fire flashed from his eyes, and flaming rocks hurtled from his mouth. When he came rushing towards Olympus, the gods fled in terror to Egypt, where they disguised themselves as animals." (Robert Graves, *The Greek Myths* [Mt. Kisco, NY: Moyer Bell Ltd.], 1988, p. 134.)

p. 110 *fathered upon Echidna . . . :* Echidna and Typhon, we are told, were also the parents of more such "dreadful brood: namely, Cerberus, the three-headed Hound of Hell, . . . the Chimæra, a fire-breathing goat with lion's head and serpent's body, and Orthrus, the two-headed hound of Geryon, who lay with his own mother and begot on her the Sphinx and the Nemean Lion." *Ibid.*

P. 110 *"Hera [Juno] reared it"*: Graves, *Ibid.*

P. 112 *[the Jinn] "shall die before the . . . resurrection"*: Lane, *Arabian Society*, p. 33.

P. 112 *further information on the Jinn: Ibid.*, p. 28.

P. 112 *"They often ascend . . .": Ibid.*, pp. 37–38.

P. 113 *Iblis is their sire and leader:* This statement, and virtually the entirety of the foregoing two or three paragraphs, are translated and/or paraphrased by Borges from Lane's *Arabian Society*, passages throughout the chapter on "Demonology."

P. 114 *"Now beneath the Fertile-Land-of-Reed-Plains"*: Post Wheeler, *The Sacred Scriptures of the Japanese*, New York: Henry Schuman, 1952, p. 90.

P. 114 *"the Jinshin-Uwo": Ibid.*, p. 495.

P. 116 *Wm. Morris' fire-being:* William Morris, *The Earthly Paradise: A Poem*, in four vols., New York: Longmans, Green, & Co., 1905, Vol. IV, p. 210.

P. 118 *Tennyson's "The Kraken":* Alfred, Lord Tennyson, *The Complete Poetical Works of Tennyson*, Boston: Houghton-Mifflin (Cambridge Edition), 1898, p. 6.

P. 120 *Damascius of Syria on the monster Kronos:* No English version of this work exists, so far as I have been able to discover; the French version seems, then, to be the one that Borges would have consulted for this entry: Damascius *"le Diadoque," Problèmes et Solutions touchant les Premiers Principes*, trans. A.-Ed. Chaignet, Paris, 1898, ¶ 123*bis*, pp. 123–24. My translation is taken from that standard text.

P. 123 *Burton's story of the Lamia:* Robert Burton, *Anatomy of Melancholy, Now for the First Time with the Latin Complete Given in Translation and Embodied in an All-English Text*, ed. Floyd Dell and Paul Jordan-Smith, New York: Tudor Publishers, 1927, p. 648.

P. 127 *"The Offspring of Leviathan":* The Golden Legend of Jacobus de Voragine [*Legenda aurea, La Legende dorée*], trans. and adapted by Granger Ryan and Helmut Ripperger, New York: Arno Press, 1969 (reprint of New York: Longmans, Green, 1941), p. 392.

P. 129 *the Mandrake's name and symbolism:* Browne, *Pseudodoxia*, Vol. I, p. 143.

P. 129 *"the white Mandragora":* For the quotations from both Pliny and Flavius Josephus, Pliny, V: 138. When the plant is pulled out of the ground, the animal dies, but the plant's leaves may be used for narcotic, magical, and laxative purposes.

P. 129 *the Mandrake at the foot of gallows:* Browne, Vol. I, p. 143.

P. 130 *the Mandrake in* The Odyssey: Homer, *The Odyssey,* trans. Robert Fitzgerald, Garden City, NY: Doubleday Anchor, 1963, X: ll. 310–14, p. 174.

P. 131 *Pliny on the Manticore:* Pliny, II: 280.

P. 131 *Flaubert on the Mantichore:* Flaubert, *op.cit.,* p. 158.

P. 134 *"The Ink Monkey":* The Chinaman Abroad: An Account of the Malayan Archipelago, particularly of Java, Ong-Tae-Hae [Wang Tai-hai], trans. W. H. Medhurst, London: John Snow (Paternoster Row), 1850, p. 46.

P. 136 *Flaubert on the Myrmecoleon:* Flaubert, *op.cit.,* p. 160.

P. 136 *The Physiologus on the Ant-Lion:* T. H. White, *The Book of Beasts: Being a Translation from a Latin Bestiary of the Twelfth Century,* New York: Dover, 1984 (repr. of New York: G. P. Putnam's Sons, 1954), p. 214*n*. It appears that there is an error in the White translation of the first sentence of this passage, which reads: "It had the face (or forepart) of a lion and the hinder parts of an ant." JLB seems to have got it right. The text here interpolates JLB's phrasing of the first sentence quoted from the Physiologus into the quotation from White's version—a hybrid. Of course, it is possible that White has it right and JLB, who often cites sources that are extremely difficult to track down with certainty, has rewritten, as he is wont to do.

P. 137 *the story of the Naga:* This story is condensed from a slightly longer version in *Buddhist Records of the Western World,* trans. "from the Chinese of Hiuen Tsiang (A. D. 629)" by Samuel Beal, Delhi: Oriental Books Reprint, 1969 (repr. of London: Trubner & Co., 1884), two volumes printed as one, Vol. II, pp. 26–27. In this book, Fa-Hsien's name is transliterated as "Fa-hian."

P. 139 *Flaubert's "Nisnas":* Flaubert, *op.cit.,* p. 156.

P. 139 *Lane's "Nesnás":* Lane, *Arabian Society,* pp. 45–46. This quotation has been edited and rearranged to conform to JLB's use of the material.

P. 143 *Odradek:* Franz Kafka, "The Cares of a Family Man," *The Penal Colony: A Country Doctor,* trans. Willa and Edwin Muir, New York: Schocken Books, 1961, pp. 160–61.

P. 145 *on the One-Eyed Creature in Góngora:* Let me quote those almost-untranslatable lines that Borges includes within the original text:

> *Un monte era de miembros eminente*
> *Este que, de Neptuno hijo fiero,*
> *De un ojo ilustra el orbe de su frente,*

Emulo casi del mayor lucero;
Cíclope a quien el pino más valiente
Bastón le obedecía tan ligero,
Y al grave peso junco tan delgado,
Que un día era bastón y otro, caiado.

Negro el cabello, imitador undoso
De las obscuras aguas del Leteo,
Al viento que le peina proceloso
Vuela sin orden, pende sin aseo;
Un torrente es su barba impetuoso
Que, adusto hijo de este Pirineo,
Su pecho inunda, o tarde o mal o en vano
Surcada aún de los dedos de su mano.

The reader can see, I hope, that from the alternate rhymes "-ente/ -ero" Góngora moves to "-eo/-oso," giving the lines a self-parodic tone; it is this "decline" to which Borges is referring in the text. Rather than attempting in a translation to reproduce this effect, and the effect of the highly ornate language generally within the verses, I have chosen simply to include the verses here and point out what Borges considers their defects.

p. 145 *Pliny on the Arimaspi:* Pliny, II: 123.

p. 146 *Herodotus on the Arimaspians:* Herodotus, *The History of Herodotus,* in two volumes, trans. G. C. Macaulay, London: Macmillan & Co., 1914, Book III, ¶ 116, p. 265.

p. 147 *Oceanus in the Iliad: The Iliad,* trans. Fitzgerald, *op.cit.,* XIV: l. 301, p. 339. Here, JLB seems to be quoting from memory, for he makes a slight error. It is not Sleep who applies this epithet to Oceanus, but Hera, or Juno. W. H. D. Rouse's prose translation concurs (*Iliad,* New York and London: Penguin Mentor Books, n.d., p. 169): "I am going to the ends of the earth. I want to see Oceanus, the father of all the gods."

p. 147 *Oceanus in Hesiod:* Hesiod, *Theogony, op.cit.,* l. 337, p. 143.

p. 147 *Fenrir's fetter:* Snorri Sturluson, *The Prose Edda of S.S.: Tales from Norse Mythology,* trans. Jean I. Young, Berkeley: University of California Press, 1954, p. 57.

p. 147 *The Mithgarth-Serpent Jörmungandr: Ibid.,* p. 56.

p. 149 *Pliny's Panther:* Pliny, VIII:23, II: 274.

p. 149 *the Panther as Christ:* The King James version would have it as "lion."

p. 149 *the Panther of an Anglo-Saxon bestiary: Codex Exoniensis* (the Exeter Code), *op.cit.*, p. 357. Here is a modern rendering of the lines in question:

> He has a singular nature,
> mild, moderate;
> he is gentle,
> kind and gracious;
> he will not aught of harm
> to any perpetrate,
> save to th'envenom'd spoiler,
> his enemy of old.

p. 149 *A twelfth-century Latin bestiary:* T. H. White, *The Book of Beasts*, p. 14. The text in White's version reads as follows:

> When a Panther has dined and is full up, it hides away in its own den and goes to sleep. After three days it wakes up again and emits a loud belch, and there comes a very sweet smell from its mouth, like the smell of allspice. When the other animals have heard the noise, they follow wherever it goes, because of the sweetness of this smell. But the Dragon only, hearing the sound, flees into the caves of the earth, being smitten with fear. There, unable to bear the smell, it becomes torpid and half asleep, and remains motionless, as if dead.

The Exeter Book has a more delicate description of that fragrant belch:

> On the third day when [the Panther] wakes, a lofty, sweet, ringing sound comes from his mouth, and with the song a most delightful stream of sweet-smelling breath, more grateful than all the blooms of herbs and blossoms of the trees. (Quoted in the Stopford Brooke translation by White, p. 14.)

The Thorpe translation is somewhat fuller:

> When the bold animal/ rises up,/ gloriously endow'd,/ on the third day,/ suddenly from sleep,/ a sound comes,/ of voices sweetest,/ through the wild-beast's mouth;/ after the voice/ an odour comes out/ from the plain,/ a steam more grateful,/ sweeter and

stronger/ than every perfume,/ than blooms of plants,/ and forest leaves,/ nobler than all/ earth's ornaments. (358)

p. 150 *the Panther of Leonardo da Vinci: The Notebooks of Leonardo da Vinci, Arranged, Rendered into English and Introduced by Edward MacCurdy,* in two volumes, New York: Reynal & Hitchcock, n.d. (prob. 1935), © 1923, repr. of orig. 1906 edition, Vol. II, "A Bestiary," p. 481.

p. 152 *the Pelican of Leonardo da Vinci: Ibid.,* p. 474.

p. 157 *Herodotus' description of the Phoenix:* Herodotus, *The History, op.cit.,* II: 73.

p. 160 *Confucius speaking:* Confucius, *The Analects,* trans. with an introduction by D. C. Lau, New York: Dorset Press, 1979, p. 86.

p. 160 *the Chart:* Confucius' translator, Mr. Lau, tells us in a note (p. 97) that both the Phoenix and the Chart were thought to be auspicious omens.

p. 160 *the bold atheist Wang Ch'ung:* reported in Willoughby-Meade, *op. cit.,* pp. 348–49.

p. 164 *the Quyata:* Lane, *Arabian Society,* p. 106.

p. 165 *the Remora of Pliny:* Pliny (IX, 41 [25]), II: 412–14.

p. 166 *further comment from Pliny on the Remora:* Pliny (XXXII: 1), VI: 2.

p. 166 *yet further comment:* Pliny (XXXII: 1), VI: 2.

p. 167 *"A Reptile Dreamed by C. S. Lewis":* C. S. Lewis, *Perelandra, op. cit.,* pp. 207–208.

p. 168 *Marco Polo's description of the Roc: The Book of Ser Marco Polo the Venetian Concerning the Kingdoms and Marvels of the East,* in two volumes, trans. and ed. by Col. Sir Henry Yule ("revised in the light of recent discoveries by Henri Cordier of Paris"), New York: Chas. Scribner's Sons, 1903, Vol. II, p. 412–13. The last sentence of Borges' text states that the feather was brought back from China, but in neither this English version nor the Penguin Classics version by R. E. Latham (Harmondsworth, Middlesex: Penguin Books, 1958, p. 274–75) does that phrase appear. In the Latham edition, in fact, the entire incident is omitted, relegated to a footnote that questions the authenticity of the statement and its inclusion in Ramusio's Italian edition of the *Travels,* itself based on a corrupt Venetian edition. Ramusio was used as a basis for many translations; if JLB was quoting from an English version, it is likely to have been Marsden's, first published in 1818, revised in 1854, and frequently reprinted. Marsden's was based entirely on Ramusio's, but I have not been able to check it for this phrase. If Borges was quoting from a Spanish version, it has been unavailable to me. Therefore, I give the phrase as the English reader today might most likely have encountered it, even though from a 1903 edition; the later, "standard" edition, simply disdains it.

P. 171 *the Salamander of Pliny:* Pliny, II: 546; V: 398.

P. 171 *the Pyrausta of Pliny:* Pliny, III: 42.

P. 172 *the Salamander of St. Augustine:* St. Augustine, *The City of God Against the Pagans,* in seven vols., with an English translation by William M. Green, Cambridge, MA: Harvard University Press (Loeb Classical Library), 1972.

P. 173 *the report of the Salamander from Marco Polo:* Marco Polo, trans. Latham, *op. cit.,* pp. 58–59.

P. 173 *the Salamander as reported by Benvenuto Cellini: The Life of Benvenuto Cellini,* trans. John Addington Symonds, 2 vols., London: John C. Nimmo, 1888, pp. 10–11.

P. 178 *The Sea Horse as described by Wang Tai-hai: The Chinaman Abroad,* Ong-Tae-Hae [Wang Tai-hai], trans. W. H. Medhurst, *op. cit.,* p. 46.

P. 179 *Pliny's description of the impregnation of mares by the wind:* Pliny, II: 322.

P. 180 *The Eight-Forked-Serpent-of-Koshi:* The material for the description of this creature is taken from Wheeler, *The Sacred Scriptures of the Japanese,* pp. 34–35 and 464–65.

P. 183 *Flaubert's Simurgh:* Flaubert, *op.cit.,* pp. 40–41.

P. 185 *"Sea rovers here take joy":* Homer, *The Odyssey, op.cit.,* XII: 180–91, p. 215.

P. 188 *"brown hair and two mammae on the breast":* Thus in Bostock and Riley [viii.30 (21)], used throughout this text. JLB's source seems to have said "brown hair and [on?] the breasts likewise," but I have opted for the standard (though perhaps no less garbled) English version.

P. 190 *The Squonk:* William T. Cox, *Fearsome Creatures of the Lumberwoods, With a Few Desert and Mountain Beasts,* illus. Coert DuBois, Washington, D.C.: Judd & Detweiler, 1910 [1911], p. 31.

P. 193 *the man of gleaming metal:* Burton, *Thousand and One Nights,* Night 15, Vol. I, p. 162. Here, JLB garbles the story somewhat; it is the brass horseman atop the Lodestone Mountain who wears a plate of lead around his neck, graven with mystic signs. The oarsman is "gleaming metal," and clearly demonic, in that as soon as the Kalandar mentions the name of Allah ("Praise Allah I am saved!") the boat and oarsman sink, leaving the Kalandar abandoned on the surface of the sea; and yet there is no mention of the leaden plate. JLB could, of course, have been remembering another edition of the *Arabian Nights;* he was familiar with at least two other English-language translations as well as the famous Galland translation into French; for an essay on the translations, see JLB, *Selected Non-Fictions,* ed. Eliot Weinberger, "The Translators of *The Thousand and One Nights,*" trans. Esther Allen, pp. 92–109.

P. 193 *Kalandar:* A Kalandar is a mendicant; in this section of the *Thousand and One Nights,* three Kalandars come to the door of a house; each one is blind in the left eye, and each is the son of a King, though each of the three comes from a different country (Burton, Vol. 1, p. 126).

P. 194 *The T'ao-T'ieh:* G. Willoughby-Meade, *op. cit.,* p. 144.

P. 195 *Thermal Beings:* Rudolf Steiner, *An Outline of Occult Science,* Spring Valley, NY: Anthroposophic Press, 1972, pp. 118–19.

P. 200 *Pliny on the Monoceros:* Pliny, II: 281.

P. 200 *Sindbad's report of the Unicorn:* Burton, *Thousand and One Nights,* Vol. II, p. 2030.

P. 201 *the battle of the Lion and the Unicorn:* These are the apposite lines in *The Faërie Queene* (Bk. II, Canto V, Stanza X):

> Like as a Lyon, whose imperiall powre
> A prowd rebellious Unicorn defyes,
> T'avoide the rash assault and wrathful stowre
> Of his fiers foe, him to a tree applyes,
> And when him ronning in full course he spyes,
> He slips aside; the whiles that furious beast
> His precious horne, sought of his enimyes,
> Strikes in the stocke, ne thence can be releast,
> But to the mighty victor yields a bounteous feast.

P. 201 *the capture of the Unicorn:* T. H. White, *op. cit.,* p. 21.

P. 201 *Leonardo on the Unicorn's sensuality:* Leonardo, *op. cit.,* p. 473.

P. 202 *the augury of the Chinese Unicorn:* G. Willoughby-Meade, *op. cit.,* p. 140.

P. 203 *the judicial Unicorn:* Ibid. p. 140

P. 203 *Margouliès' Unicorn:* G[eorges] Margouliès, *Anthologie Raisonnée de la Littérature Chinoise,* Paris: Payot, 1948, pp. 120–21. The ninth-century author of this piece, which I have translated from the French, is given as "Han Yu."

P. 207 *"We are all cheated by the floating pile":* Ariosto, *Orlando Furioso, op. cit.,* VI: 37, p. 90.

P. 208 *the isle Jasconius: The Voyage of Saint Brendan: Journey to the Promised Land* ["Navigatio Sancti Brendani Abbatis"], trans. with an introd. by John J. O'Meara, Dublin: Dolmen Press, 1976, pp. 18–19.

AVAILABLE FROM PENGUIN CLASSICS

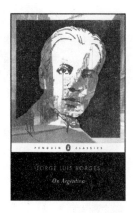  

On Argentina

On Mysticism

On Writing

Collected Fictions

Selected Non-Fictions

Selected Poems

The Aleph and Other Stories

The Book of Sand and
Shakespeare's Memory

Brodie's Report

A Universal History of Iniquity

Poems of the Night

The Sonnets

PENGUIN CLASSICS

NOW AVAILABLE

The poems, essays, and collected fiction of one of the
20th century's greatest writers, Jorge Luis Borges

The Book of Sand and
Shakespeare's Memory
ISBN 978-0-14-310529-9

Brodie's Report
ISBN 978-0-14-303925-9

A Universal History of Iniquity
ISBN 978-0-14-243789-6

The Aleph and Other Stories
ISBN 978-0-14-243788-9

Available in Penguin Classics Deluxe Editions:

The Book of Imaginary Beings
ISBN 978-0-14-303993-8

Collected Fictions
ISBN 978-0-14-028680-9

Selected Non-Fictions
ISBN 978-0-14-029011-0

Selected Poems
ISBN 978-0-14-058721-0

PENGUIN CLASSICS